Lacey averted her eyes from the erotic carvings

"Do they shock you?" Marcus asked.

"No," she replied hesitantly, sliding her gaze back to the relief carvings on the temple walls. "They're really very...beautiful." And so they were, all these exquisitely carved bodies in various forms of physical adoration. "But why here, in a temple?"

"The primitive Nepalese religions revered fertility and the continuation of life, which the sexual act represents," he said.

Lacey felt the unease that had haunted her earlier return in full force. She glanced up nervously at Marcus. His slate-gray eyes were quite unreadable, but something about the fixed line of his mouth warned her that Marcus was a very long way from being the cool, detached man she had worked for these past months....

JOANNA MANSELL finds writing hard work but very addictive. When she's not bashing away at her typewriter, she's usually got her nose buried in a book. She also loves gardening and daydreaming, two pastimes that go together remarkably well. The ambition of this Essex-born author is to write books that people will enjoy reading.

Books by Joanna Mansell

HARLEQUIN ROMANCE
2836—THE NIGHT IS DARK
2866—SLEEPING TIGER
2894—BLACK DIAMOND

JOANNA MANSELL

miracle man

Harlequin Books

TORONTO • NEW YORK • LONDON
AMSTERDAM • PARIS • SYDNEY • HAMBURG
STOCKHOLM • ATHENS • TOKYO • MILAN

Harlequin Presents first edition October 1988
ISBN 0-373-11116-9

Original hardcover edition published in 1987
by Mills & Boon Limited

CHAPTER ONE

'YOU want me to learn Nepali?'

Lacey Harrison stared rather suspiciously at the man sitting on the other side of the desk. As always, though, his face was quite unreadable. What was that old saying about the eyes being the mirror of the soul? But then, after a year of working for Marcus Caradin, she was convinced he didn't *have* a soul.

'Nepali?' she repeated, a slightly edgy note creeping into her voice now. 'Why on earth do you want me to learn an outlandish language like that?'

The cool grey gaze of her boss rested on her assessingly. She always found it rather disconcerting when he fixed his full attention on her like this, and she shifted uneasily in her chair.

'I'd have thought that was perfectly obvious,' he answered smoothly. 'I'm planning a trip to Nepal in the near future, and I intend to take you with me.'

That was what she had been afraid of from the moment when he had first broached the subject. Her mouth set into a stubborn line, and she sat up very straight.

'I'm really not interested in getting involved with trips abroad,' she told him firmly. 'I much prefer working here, in the office.'

He didn't answer straight away, but just kept looking at her in that assessing manner which, for some reason, was starting to make her nerves jangle. What was going on inside that clever head of his? she wondered a little

5

crossly. She didn't know, she had never been able to guess what he was thinking, what he was feeling.

It was nearly a year now since Marcus Caradin had bought out the financially ailing company of Worldwide Travel, and re-launched it under the name of Caradin Tours. During that time, he had always remained distant; in fact, he treated her more like a valuable piece of office equipment than a personal secretary. Their relationship was strictly formal and impersonal, beginning and ending at the office door. Not that she minded—definitely not! It was an attitude which suited her right down to the ground.

For an instant, her mind flicked back to the moment when he had first walked into the office, nearly a year ago. He had briefly introduced himself, then immediately turned to a stack of files on the desk. 'Let's make a start on this backlog of correspondence,' he had said crisply, and had at once started to dictate at a speed that had sent her pencil fairly flying over the pages of her notebook.

She—and all the rest of the staff—had worked flat out for the next few months. Worldwide Travel had been in deep trouble when Marcus Caradin had bought it, seriously under-capitalised, and with an old-fashioned image. He had immediately set out to change all that and, exhausted though she often was during those first gruelling few weeks, she grudgingly acknowledged that he worked harder than any of them as they fought to save the travel firm from going under.

'We need a totally new approach,' Marcus Caradin had told them at the staff meeting he had called on the day after his arrival. 'We can't go on offering the Costa del Sol type of holidays, we simply can't compete with the big travel companies who can negotiate large discounts and undercut our prices. That's why I intend to

concentrate on offering a more exotic range of holidays.
Caradin Tours will specialise in the type of holiday that
isn't offered by the big tour operators. There's a fast-
growing market in this area, a lot of people are looking
for something different, something more adventurous
than a couple of weeks lazing under the Spanish sun.
Caradin Tours will cater to that need, we'll take them to
some of the most remote, most interesting parts of the
world.'

Privately, Lacey had thought he was quite mad. She
predicted to herself that Caradin Tours would collapse in
a few months, and began to scan the 'situations vacant'
columns in the papers, certain she would be needing a
new job in the very near future. Craving stability and
security in her own life, she couldn't imagine why anyone
would want to spend their precious couple of weeks'
holiday suffering discomfort, often primitive living
conditions, even danger, just to visit some distant corner
of the world. To her astonishment, though, it turned out
there were large numbers of people who just couldn't
wait to book such a holiday.

In the beginning, Caradin Tours had only been able to
offer a fairly limited range of holidays. Finance had been
tight, even though Marcus Caradin had invested a large
sum of his own money in the company, and of course it
took a great deal of time and organisation to set up each
individual tour. Initial returns had been good, though,
and the demand for the holidays had been far greater
than anyone—except perhaps Marcus Caradin himself—had expected. They were gradually widening their
range, now. It was possible to travel with Caradin Tours
across the hot sands of the Sahara, to some of the wildest
parts of Africa, even to the frozen North.

Not that Lacey ever regarded them as *holidays*.

Endurance tests—that was how she privately described them to herself. And there was no way on earth she would willingly go on one of those trips herself.

But now her boss was sitting opposite her and calmly telling her that he intended to take her with him to Nepal. Perhaps he would be willing to listen to a reasonable argument, she told herself hopefully. She could think of half a dozen perfectly good excuses why she shouldn't go with him, and she was just about to try a couple out on him when he held up one hand.

'My decision isn't open to discussion,' he informed her coolly.

Lacey tried to keep the frustration out of her eyes. Was the man a mind-reader? This wasn't the first time in their working relationship that he had seemed to know exactly what she was about to say, and had stepped in to forestall her.

'But *why* do you want me to go with you?' she asked, deciding she was at least entitled to know that.

He relaxed back in his chair. 'You're an extremely efficient secretary,' he said, after a brief pause. 'Probably the most efficient I've ever had.' Her eyebrows shot up at that; Marcus Caradin's compliments were about as rare as dodos' eggs. 'You're also a very intelligent girl, Lacey,' he went on, astonishing her even further. 'You're good at dealing with people, you cope well in a crisis, and over the past year I've found you to be totally reliable. In short, I think we're not using you to your full potential. You'd be of far more use to this company if you took on more responsibility.' He leant forward a little, and those grey eyes were fixed on her again now, sending an unfamiliar quiver running through all her nerve-ends. 'This is what I'm proposing. You'll continue to be my personal secretary, but I'll employ another girl to deal with the routine typing and office work. In future, you'll deal only with confidential correspondence and reports. That will leave you free to accompany me on trips abroad, so you can learn how to set up new holiday tours and cope with the hundred and one administrative problems that always crop up. If everything works out well, when you've finally gained enough experience, you can branch out on your own and take over this entire side of the business.'

Lacey felt her mouth dropping open. This was even worse than she had expected! He intended that she should eventually do this on a permanent basis.

In the past, Marcus Caradin had always undertaken these preliminary trips himself, travelling abroad at regular intervals to whatever far corner of the world he had decided would prove a popular holiday destination. Before any holiday could be offered to the public, a lot of behind-the-scenes work had to be done. Hotel bookings had to be arranged, local travel facilities investigated, an itinerary drawn up of all the local tourist spots worth visiting, and a whole host of minor details dealt with.

Now he was telling her that, once she was experienced enough, she would be the one who would deal with this side of things, travelling all over the place, and living out of a suitcase. And he was looking at her expectantly now, as if waiting for her to stammer out her gratitude for giving her this fantastic opportunity. It was clear that he considered he was offering her a job that any girl in her right mind would jump at without hesitation.

Well, not her! But she had a feeling it wouldn't go down too well if she came right out and told him that. Although Lacey often felt that she didn't know Marcus Caradin any better now than she had on that morning when he had first strode into the office, there was one thing she had very quickly found out about him. Once he had made a firm decision about something, it was more or less impossible to persuade him to change his mind. And he seemed very determined that she should take on this new job. On the other hand, she was equally determined that she didn't want to do it, and she wasn't going to give up without a fight.

She raised her head and looked straight at him. 'What if I said I wasn't interested? That I'd much prefer to remain just your personal secretary?'

A quick flash of displeasure instantly registered in his slate-grey eyes. Lacey had seen that reaction before, and she swallowed nervously. She was well aware that her boss didn't like to be crossed. Although in many ways he was a scrupulously fair man, this company belonged to him, he ran it exactly as he wanted to run it, and he had made it perfectly clear from the very beginning that anyone who disagreed with his long-term aims and plans had better start looking for another job.

His gaze was very level now, and had gone decidedly cool. 'I wouldn't want to lose you, Lacey,' he stated pointedly. 'Perhaps you should think my proposal over very carefully.'

That was blackmail! Lacey thought furiously to herself. She wished she had the nerve to jump to her feet, fling his offer straight back at him, then stalk out. The trouble was, jobs weren't so easy to find nowadays and he knew that, he was trading on that fact, damn him. And anyway, she didn't really *want* to give in her notice.

The truth was, she and Marcus Caradin were curiously well suited. They both left their personal lives behind them as soon as they stepped into the office, and that made for an easy, undemanding working relationship. When he had first arrived, there had been rumours of a

recent and rather messy divorce, and she had purposefully closed her ears to the gossip; she hadn't wanted to
know any details. And although she had been well aware
that he was initially a little annoyed by the fact that she
was only in her early twenties, that he would have much
preferred a more mature woman as his personal
secretary, she had set out to be ultra-efficient and
indispensable, and she had apparently succeeded, because he had never made any attempt to replace her.

It hadn't taken her long to realise that nearly everyone
in the company was waiting for a red-hot affair to spring
up between the two of them. She had had to put up with
endless insinuations about her new boss, she had been
half amused, half exasperated to discover that they were
even taking bets on how long it would be before she
succumbed to his charms.

Because there was one fact that was quite indisput-
able. Marcus Caradin was absolutely gorgeous. Those
soulless eyes, his bright gold hair, the long, lean body clad
in impeccably cut suits; and perhaps most lethal of all,
that aura of tightly reined sexuality, all the more potent
because it was never blatant, never obvious, only
revealing itself in brief but quite devastating flashes.

Lacey knew perfectly well that she was the only female
in the entire company unaffected by it. She also knew
that most of the other girls would have cheerfully
committed murder to get her job and the chance to work
alongside Marcus Caradin. And she regularly gave up a
small prayer of thanks that she was totally immune to his
particular brand of attractiveness. She had known too
many Marcus Caradins in her life; she had long ago
become totally turned off by all that male virility, she was
an expert at recognising it for what it was—an empty
promise of a pleasure that, at best, was only fleeting, at

worst utterly humiliating.

But now he had thrown this bombshell at her. She wasn't worried by the prospect of travelling abroad with him, she was sure she could cope with that perfectly well. It was just that she didn't want to travel at all, she had done quite enough of that all her life. It had been sheer bliss these past couple of years, having a settled home, a regular routine, a steady nine-to-five job. All right, so a lot of people would have considered it boring. To her, though, it had been a much-prized luxury, and so far she had relished every minute of it.

Only now Marcus Caradin had stepped in and completely ruined it. Nor was he giving her any choice; she could either fall in with his plans or start looking for another job. And quite apart from the fact that she didn't relish the thought of the long trudge around the employment agencies, there was the financial side of it to be considered. She earned a good salary, but the cost of living in London was high, there was nothing much left at the end of each month, and her bank balance was depressingly low. She couldn't afford to walk out, at least not until she had another job lined up.

She gave a tiny sigh of frustration, then her shoulders sagged in a clear gesture of defeat.

'It doesn't look as if I've got a lot of choice, does it?'

Marcus Caradin looked at her rather sharply. 'I thought you would welcome the chance to break away from a routine office job. And it *is* a promotion, there'll be a higher salary to go with it.'

'Thank you,' she said, without much enthusiasm. 'Well, if I've got to go to Nepal with you, perhaps you'd better fill me in on some of the details.'

He shot a dark frown in her direction, as if he couldn't figure out why she wasn't thrilled and excited at his proposal. Then he turned away, and took a map out from the drawer in his desk. Spreading the map out on the desk-top, he gestured to her to come and take a look at it.

'This new tour I've got in mind will start in India,' he told her, his tone brisk and businesslike again now. 'I thought we'd fly the tour parties out to Delhi, let them have two or three days exploring the city, then shunt them across four hundred and fifty miles of northern India by rail.' He glanced up, and his lean mouth relaxed in a rare smile. 'Travelling by railway in India is an experience in itself,' he added drily. 'And one thing I've learnt in this last year is that our clients love a challenge. The more difficult and demanding the journey, the more they seem to enjoy it. So, we'll take them by rail to Varanasi in north-east India, then by coach across the border into Nepal, and on to Kathmandu.'

For a few moments, Lacey found herself unexpectedly fascinated by the sight of his long, tanned finger moving over the map, tracing out the route. She stared at his well shaped nails, and absently noted how strong his wrist looked. Then his voice broke into her wandering thoughts, and she hurriedly pulled herself together again.

'After they've spent three or four days sight-seeing in Kathmandu, we'll offer them the optional extra of a trek on foot through the foothills of the Himalayas to the town of Pokhara,' he went on. 'The trek will probably take several days, as they'll have to travel at the pace of the slowest in the party. A couple of days in Pokhara for a short rest and some more sight-seeing, then the coach back to Kathmandu, and from there we'll fly them home to England. How does that sound to you?'

Like a holiday for masochists, she thought gloomily to herself. She didn't quite have the nerve to say it out loud, though, so she fixed an enthusiastic smile on to her face and tried hard to look interested.

'It sounds—fine,' she said, somehow managing to keep her voice bright.

'I think it'll certainly prove a very popular holiday,' he agreed with a nod of satisfaction. 'And the initial arrangements shouldn't be too difficult, we shouldn't be gone for more than a couple of weeks. Now, let's get down to details. Here's a list of the inoculations you'll need,' he said, handing her a sheet of paper, 'and this is the address of Mr Thapa, who's agreed to give you a few basic lessons in Nepali. You can leave early each afternoon in order to attend the lessons. I'll arrange for one of the other girls to come in and cover for you while you're away from the office.'

Her mouth curved into an involuntary smile. She could imagine the frantic scramble there would be to be the one chosen to work in Marcus Caradin's office for a couple of precious hours each afternoon. Then the smile faded away again, and her brows wrinkled slightly.

'Er—exactly *why* do I have to learn Nepali?'

'I'd have thought that was fairly obvious. One of us should know at least a few basic phrases.'

'But won't there be quite a lot of people who speak English in Kathmandu?' she asked. 'After all, it's quite a tourist centre now, isn't it?'

'Yes, it is. But I don't think we can count on finding people who speak English once we leave Kathmandu and start out on the trek to Pokhara.'

Lacey stared at him in dismay. 'We've got to do the trek as well?' she squeaked.

The first signs of impatience began to show on his normally well controlled features.

'That *is* one of the reasons the two of us are going on

this trip, to cover the whole tour ourselves first, to see if it's feasible.'

'Well yes—but——' she floundered.

'We'll do the proposed holiday ourselves, from beginning to end,' he reminded her a little tersely. 'We'll inspect local hotels, try out different travel facilities, make arrangements with local coach operators where necessary, and generally prepare all the groundwork for the tour. Once we reach Kathmandu, we'll need to do the trek to Pokhara, mainly to make sure that it's physically possible, bearing in mind that a lot of the people who'll eventually book this holiday will be middle-aged or even older. Provided we find it's not impossibly strenuous, we'll then need to work out roughly how far it's feasible to travel each day, and to make sure there are plenty of rest-houses along the route, so the tour parties can be certain of having somewhere to sleep each night.'

The thought of slogging on foot through the Himalayas didn't thrill her in the least, she would definitely have preferred to have been curled up in front of the television in her cosy little flat, or to be having a quiet dinner at one of the local restaurants with Robert.

'Provided everything goes smoothly and we can fix up all the administrative details, we'll start advertising the tour as soon as we get back,' Marcus continued. 'I fully expect it to be one of our most popular tours next year. As a matter of fact,' he added unexpectedly, 'I'm rather looking forward to this particular trip. I think it could well be quite an experience.'

'I'm sure it will be,' agreed Lacey, and she hoped he couldn't hear the note of deep depression in her voice.

'Nepali is an impossible language,' Lacey announced to her flat-mate in total exasperation.

Jane was lounging on a sofa, flicking through a magazine. 'I'm sure Mr Caradin doesn't expect you to be fluent, not in just a couple of weeks. Just a few basic phrases—that's what you said he wanted, wasn't it?'

'But you don't understand, it's full of absolutely unpronounceable sounds. Anyway, Mr Thapa says there are dozens of different dialects. Probably no one will understand a single word I say,' she predicted gloomily.

Jane gave a small sigh. 'Honestly, Lacey, I don't know why you're making all this fuss. You're going off on this fantastic holiday with Marcus Caradin—Marcus Caradin,' she repeated, her eyes taking on a rather glazed, dreamy look as she savoured each syllable of his name, 'and all you can do is complain all the time.'

'Well, that might have something to do with the fact that I don't want to go,' retorted Lacey, scowling balefully at the Nepali phrase-book in her hand. 'And it is *not* a holiday, Marcus Caradin won't be any less of a slave-driver than he is in the office, you can bet on that.'

'But you'll be wandering through all those exotic places together,' Jane pointed out enviously. 'Hand in hand under the hot eastern sun, long nights in remote little hotels——' She gave a small shiver just at the thought of it. 'Anything could happen under those circumstances.'

Jane also worked at Caradin Tours, in the accounts department, and Lacey was getting thoroughly tired of being constantly reminded how lucky she was to be working for the gorgeous Marcus Caradin. Rather irritably, she ran her fingers through the dark red strands of her hair, released now from the decorative clips which kept it tidily in place during the day.

'I can tell you precisely what'll happen,' she stated firmly. 'Absolutely nothing!'

Jane sighed again. 'Sometimes I think you've got no

romance in your soul.'

'As far as I'm concerned, that's a compliment,' Lacey shot back instantly. 'I don't need romance in my life; all I want is a steady job, a warm, comfortable flat to come back to in the evenings, and an occasional night out with Robert.'

Jane shook her head slightly despairingly. 'That's not living, that's just existing! There are times when I just don't understand you, Lacey.' Then, seeing the warning glint in Lacey's green eyes, she shrugged. 'All right, I'll drop the subject—for now. What are you doing tonight? Going out with Robert?'

'No, he's gone away for a few days. Some business conference up in Scotland.'

'I don't know why you keep going out with Robert,' Jane said, wrinkling her nose slightly. 'He's not right for you, Lacey, you know he isn't. He's too old, too staid, too—well, too boring,' she finished bluntly.

'He's just old-fashioned, that's all,' answered Lacey, quite unperturbed, and not in the least offended. In fact, that was precisely why she enjoyed going out with him. Robert would never spring any surprises on her, he always behaved like a perfect gentleman. He fitted in very well with the orderly life-style she had carved out for herself these past couple of years.

'Do you want to come out with Phil and me?' invited Jane. 'We're going to try out that new nightclub that's just opened.'

'No, thanks. Two's company, three's definitely a crowd. Anyway,' went on Lacey with a grimace, 'I'd better stick with the phrase-book a bit longer. Unless I can ask where the toilets are in half a dozen different dialects, we could be in real trouble.'

She struggled with the phrase book for another couple

of hours, then finally tossed it aside in exasperation and made herself a late supper. Once it was eaten and cleared away, she turned on the television and settled down to watch a late film.

It was just past midnight when Jane came waltzing back in. 'We had a fantastic evening, I really enjoyed it. And guess who was at the club? Marcus Caradin!' she went on, without giving Lacey a chance to answer. 'And he had this tall, stunning blonde with him, just the sort you'd expect him to take out. Have you ever seen any of his girlfriends before? Is this one a regular?'

'I've no idea,' answered Lacey a little curtly, wishing Jane would shut up and let her watch the end of the film.

But Jane wouldn't let it alone. 'Haven't any of them ever rung him up at work? Come on, they must have done. I bet he doesn't live like a monk, he's probably got a whole string of women chasing after him.'

With odd reluctance, Lacey found herself remembering the husky-voiced women who occasionally phoned up and asked to be put through to Marcus Caradin. She had never paid much attention to them, though, briskly connecting them and then not giving them another thought. For a few moments, she wondered if one of those voices belonged to the beautiful blonde Jane had seen with her boss tonight. Then she swiftly clamped down on that particular line of thought. Either way, it was absolutely no concern of hers.

She got to her feet and switched off the television, the film forgotten. 'I've no idea what Marcus Caradin does in his private life. He could have a whole harem of women for all I know—or care.' She yawned rather ostentatiously, as if totally bored with the subject. 'I'm tired, I'm going to bed. See you in the morning, Jane.'

And she had been sure she really *was* tired, yet

somehow she couldn't seem to sleep, she just dozed fitfully, and finally crawled out of bed next morning feeling heavy-eyed and irritable. Her hair wouldn't go right, bright red strands stuck out all over her head, and she burnt her fingers on the curling-tongs as she tried to coax them back into place. Then she couldn't find a pair of tights that weren't laddered, and to cap it all, the battered Mini she and Jane shared wouldn't start; they finally had to push it to get it going.

She eventually arrived at Caradin Tours feeling hot and flustered. A quick glance at her watch told her she was several minutes late, and she let out a small groan. She was all too aware of Marcus Caradin's views on unpunctuality. When she reached her own office, though, there was no sign of him, and the switchboard operator rang through a few minutes later to say he had left a message that he wouldn't be in until mid-morning.

Lacey slumped down at her desk and let out a rueful sigh. All that rushing about for nothing. She took the cover off her typewriter, and set to work on some letters she hadn't had time to finish the previous afternoon.

For some reason, though, she seemed to be all fingers and thumbs. By mid-morning she hadn't managed more than half a dozen letters, and she was just muttering under her breath at yet another typing mistake when the outer door of the office suddenly opened, making her jump slightly.

'Get a grip on yourself, Lacey,' she murmured under her breath, wondering why on earth she was so edgy this morning. Then she lifted her head and crisply greeted her boss as he strode into the office.

He paused at her desk to pick up a couple of reports lying there, and as he quickly leafed through them, she studied him from under slightly lowered lashes. The gold hair somehow seemed even brighter this morning. It really wasn't fair, Lacey thought to herself, most girls would have given just about anything to have had hair that colour. Come to think of it, it should have looked wrong on a man, and yet it certainly didn't look wrong on Marcus Caradin—far from it. In fact, it looked—well, rather stunning, she concluded. Not that it had the slightest effect on her, of course it didn't, she reminded herself rather hastily. But other women didn't seem quite as immune to its dazzling brilliance, she had seen how their gazes were drawn to it, sometimes lingering there for ages.

Her gaze drifted down over the dark suit, the immaculate white shirt, then lifted to his face again. Were those fresh shadows of tiredness under the usually too-alert slate-grey eyes? she found herself wondering. Had that tall blonde Jane had seen him with last night found some way of stirring up all that cool detachment into a white-hot fever?

Utterly astonished by the direction her thoughts were taking, Lacey flushed hotly, then hurriedly wound a fresh sheet of paper into the typewriter and began pounding away at top speed. What on earth had made her think of such a thing? Whatever Marcus Caradin did or didn't get up to with his girlfriends, it was certainly no business of hers!

Much to her relief, things soon seemed to return to normal and the rest of the day passed without incident. Late in the afternoon, Marcus came out to give her a folder of letters he had signed, then he glanced at his watch and frowned slightly.

'Shouldn't you have left? I thought your lesson in Nepali started at four.'

Lacey gave a small groan. 'I forgot all about the time.

Mr Thapa isn't going to be very pleased if I'm late.'

'How are the lessons going?'

She gave an expressive grimace. 'Don't ask! At the moment I can just about manage half a dozen short phrases, and a few basic words like yes, no, hello and goodbye.'

One of Marcus's well-shaped eyebrows lifted gently. 'Then perhaps you should begin to make a little more effort, because we'll be leaving at the end of next week.'

Lacey swallowed nervously. 'Next week?' she echoed, feeling an unexpected fluttering in her stomach.

'We'll probably be gone for about a fortnight,' continued Marcus, not seeming to notice her sudden edginess. 'I take it there won't be any problems? That you don't have any——' he paused delicately for a moment before continuing smoothly, 'any personal relationships that will make it difficult for you to be away that length of time? I suppose I should have asked you before, but to be honest it didn't occur to me until today.'

To her annoyance, she found she had started to flush furiously again, her face seemed to be permanently red today.

'There certainly won't be any problems in that direction,' she declared and hoped she didn't sound as flustered as she felt. What was the matter with her today? Why the hell was she behaving like this? 'I do have one or two—friends,' she went on stiffly, 'but I'm a free agent, I can do exactly as I please.'

'An independent woman?' he queried in a faintly amused tone.

Was he mocking her? She couldn't be sure, she had never been able to figure out what was going on behind that controlled expression, those soulless eyes.

'I certainly value my independence,' she answered,

relieved to feel the heat slowly leaving her glowing skin. 'I don't see anything wrong in that.'

'Nor do I,' he agreed, rather to her surprise. 'In fact, I think that personal independence is something to be highly valued.' His mouth relaxed in the very faintest of smiles. 'Since we seem to think alike on so many things, there's no reason why we shouldn't be able to work as well together on this trip as we do in the office.'

'I'm sure we will,' she assured him in a voice that was now as cool and formal as his own. Deep inside, though, she could still feel a faint flutter of unease. Why were her nerves in such a rattled state today?

It was probably because of her sleepless night, she decided at last. Yet as she gathered up her jacket and left for her lesson with Mr Thapa, she suddenly found herself wishing she could go down with flu, measles, a hacking cough, anything that would give her a legitimate excuse for getting out of this trip to India and Nepal with Marcus Caradin.

CHAPTER TWO

LACEY opened her eyes, but couldn't remember where she was for several seconds. All she knew was that she was dog-tired, even after a long, deep and undisturbed sleep. Stretching her stiff, aching limbs, she blinked at the first glow of dawn filtering through the shutters of the window, then realised that she could hear the faint sound of a rhythmic drumbeat, soon joined by the melodic if slightly mournful sound of a sitar.

Memories slowly drifted back into her tired mind. This was Varanasi, in north-east India. Outside the window of her hotel room flowed the River Ganges. In fact, its distinctive smell seemed to permeate the room, not exactly unpleasant, just—well, strong, she decided with a delicate wrinkling of her nose.

And just a couple of rooms away, down the corridor, was Marcus Caradin. At the thought of her boss, her mouth set into a distinct grimace. Several times over the past year she had complained to Jane that he was a slave-driver, but compared to the last few days, life in the office at Caradin Tours had been an absolute picnic. No sooner had they arrived in Delhi than he had set out on an exhaustingly thorough exploration of the city, with her in close tow. They had tramped round the Red Fort, marvelled at the great mosque of Jama Masjid, gazed at the President's magnificent residence, and explored the bustling, colourful mechants' quarters. After Marcus had sketched out an itinerary of tourist sights which could be crammed into the proposed three-day stay in Delhi, they had then set off on the rounds of the local hotels.

Lacey had soon discovered that Marcus's standards were extremely high. They had tried well over a dozen hotels before he finally found one which seemed to meet his exacting requirements. Then they had settled down to haggle over the price of a regular block booking.

'Never accept the original price,' Marcus had instructed her briskly when the negotiations were finally over, 'especially in countries where haggling is an accepted part of any business deal.'

Rather to her annoyance, he had looked as alert and fresh as when they had first started out this morning, while she had felt as if she were positively wilting from heat and weariness. Where on earth did the man get all his energy from? she had wondered a little resentfully.

'Can we have something to eat now?' she had ventured, staring up at him hopefully.

Those cool grey eyes had registered a flicker of disapproval, as if she had suggested something outrageously frivolous.

'We're here to work, not to relax and enjoy ourselves,' he had told her rather reprovingly. 'Remember, Lacey, eventually you'll have to cope with all these details on your own.'

Not if she could help it, she had thought with growing determination. They had only been away from England for a couple of days, but she was already quite certain that this wasn't the kind of career she wanted for herself, being shunted out to all corners of the world, haggling with hotel owners and tramping for hours around the local tourist attractions. To be fair to Marcus—and herself—she wouldn't throw in the towel just yet, she would stick this particular trip out to the end. Once they were back in England again, though, she was fairly certain she would be issuing an ultimatum. Either he let her go back to being just his personal secretary, or she would start looking for a new job.

They had finally left Delhi, and the long train journey across northern India had been every bit as gruelling as Marcus had promised it would be. Hot, dusty, exhausted, and with her senses constantly bombarded with unfamiliar, exotic and often rather overwhelming smells and sounds, she had found the experience incredibly tiring and yet unexpectedly fascinating. All the same, she had been thoroughly relieved when it was finally over. Arriving at last in Varanasi, she had been too bone-weary to appreciate its jumble of towers, turrets and domes, the pinkish stonework seeming to glow under the hot rays of the sun. She had just about managed to swallow a few mouthfuls of food, then had stumbled off to bed and fallen straight into a deep, deep sleep.

Only now something had woken her up much earlier than she had intended. Lacey gave a grunt of annoyance, then turned over and determinedly closed her eyes again. She had no intention of getting up for at least another couple of hours. In fact, she might even plead a headache and stay in bed all morning.

She was just looking forward to the prospect of a long lie-in when a brisk rap on the door made her eyes flicker open again. 'Early morning tea?' she mumbled to herself, as she very reluctantly crawled out of bed. 'But I didn't order any——'

She groped sleepily for the handle and opened the door; then her eyes shot wide open because standing on the other side, fully dressed and briskly alert, was Marcus Caradin.

For a few moments they simply stared silently at each other, and she had the distinct impression that something had briefly jolted him out of his usual cool detachment. Then, to her astonishment, she realised his gaze was sliding over her tousled red hair, moving down to her shoulders, finally seeming to be drawn irresistibly, involuntarily downwards. And for the very first time she could remember, she saw a little of that bland coolness actually melt away; an unfamiliar glint of response flickered in the slaty depths of those usually unreadable eyes.

Confused and unexpectedly disturbed, she took refuge in indignation.

'Do you have any idea what time it is?' she demanded.

His own self-control instantly slid back into place. 'I always think that time's rather irrelevant in India, don't you?'

'That rather depends on your point of view,' she retorted. 'It doesn't seem particularly irrelevant if you're tired out and looking forward to another couple of hours in bed. You woke me up!'

'That *was* my intention,' he told her calmly. 'Although I didn't expect you to be such a very sound sleeper. I was beginning to think I was going to have to come in and physically haul you out of that bed.'

Lacey didn't answer straight away. In fact, she was rather alarmed to find her mind was suddenly flooded with disturbingly vivid pictures of Marcus Caradin hauling her out from under the bedclothes. She swallowed hard, trying to get her dry throat working again.

'It's some ungodly hour in the morning and I just want to get back to sleep,' she somehow managed to get out at last.

'You're awake now. Why not join me in a walk down to the river?' he suggested persuasively. 'You might as well make the most of this opportunity to see something of Varanasi, and the Ganges.'

It was a tempting offer, but a small voice in her ear was already warning her that it would be much wiser to turn it down. Although she couldn't have explained why, she definitely had the feeling that it would *not* be a good idea to go wandering off with Marcus Caradin right now. What was that joke Jane had made about the two of them walking hand in hand into the sunset? Well, the first glow of dawn could have an equally unsettling effect on all the senses, and for some reason she was feeling unusually vulnerable this morning. It was probably because she was still feeling tired, she reasoned, not properly awake yet. Anyway, whatever the reason, she just didn't feel confident that she could rely on her usual common sense to keep everything in perspective. The best thing would be to tell him, very firmly, that she didn't want to go with him.

He didn't give her a chance, though. Before she could politely turn down his invitation, he had already cut in.

'I'll be leaving in about ten minutes. Get dressed, then meet me down in the lobby—and don't keep me waiting!'

She had heard that authoritative tone so many times back in the office of Caradin Tours that she automatically jumped to obey it. It wasn't until she was hurriedly dragging a comb through her hair that she realised she didn't *have* to do what he said. When they weren't working, she was entitled to do exactly as she pleased. Old habits died hard, though, and a few minutes later she was scooting down to the lobby.

Marcus was already there, waiting for her. 'There's no time to eat,' he said, 'not if we want to be at the Ganges in time for the sunrise. We'll have breakfast when we get back.'

'Why do we have to be there at sunrise? ' she asked,

scuttling to keep up with him as he set off at a fast pace.

'You'll understand that when we get there,' he answered rather cryptically, and since he was walking even faster now, she didn't have enough breath left to ask him any more questions.

Outside, the sky was glowing eerily with the pale light of early dawn. Despite the earliness of the hour, Varanasi was already bustling with life. Cycles, rickshaws and scooters were dashing through the narrow alleyways, bells and horns sounded on all sides, while a cow completely blocked their path at one point, everyone patiently stopping and waiting until the sacred animal finally ambled off again.

The hotel was close to the river, so it didn't take them long to reach one of the main ghats, a landing stage which led right down to the river in a series of steps. Some of the noise and bustle had been left behind now, but there were still crowds of people milling about on the steps.

Lacey stood still for a moment, and stared around her in fascination. Near by, a group of pilgrims had pushed floating candles out on to the river, and the tiny lights were now bobbing their way erratically downstream while the pilgrims swayed gently in time to haunting sitar music. Other pilgrims with shaved heads and wearing only loincloths were wading out into the river and immersing themselves in the water, their hands clasped together in prayer.

'Is it like this every morning?' she asked.

'Of course. The pilgrims come here to cleanse themselves, both spiritually and bodily. To these people, the Ganges is a holy river. They believe that, at sunrise, it unites with the sun and has the power to purify them.'

'What a lovely idea,' she said softly.

'Yes, it is,' he agreed. 'Although personally, I'd rather have a shower,' he added rather drily. 'They use the river for a lot of other purposes as well!'

'Don't go into any details,' she said hurriedly. 'My stomach's always a bit delicate first thing in the morning. Anyway, it would spoil the romance of it all.'

Marcus turned to a young Indian girl who was weaving in and out of the crowd, selling marigolds, rice and tika, a crimson powder which the Hindus used in one of their ceremonies. He took a couple of coins from his pocket, then bought one of the bright orange marigolds from her.

Lacey watched him, a little puzzled. What was he doing? Before she had time to ask him, though, he had turned back to her and slid the marigold into her hair.

The unexpected gesture completely flustered her. She reached up and fingered the delicate petals of the flower, then stared at Marcus rather uncertainly.

'Why did you do that?'

'Perhaps I wanted to put the romance back into the morning for you.' There was a faintly teasing note in his voice, but there was also an odd, bright expression in his eyes that she had never seen before, and which made her feel distinctly uneasy. Then he pointed ahead of them. 'Look. The sun's coming up.'

And so it was, sliding slowly above the horizon, its rays gently touching the city and bathing it in a soft light which disguised the ancient, crumbling stonework, turning it to pink-and-gold-encrusted splendour. Then the river began to reflect the sun's glow, and for an instant the water turned blood-red, making Lacey catch her breath at the bright flash of colour.

She turned to Marcus, wanting to make sure that he hadn't missed the spectacle. And it was then that she discovered he wasn't watching the sunrise at all. Instead, he was staring straight at her.

In an instant, the crowds of people and the river were completely forgotten. The man standing beside her claimed all her attention, his tall figure touched with the same golden glow that had lit the city, his hair seeming even more brightly alive than usual. And his face—why hadn't she ever really seen it clearly before? The grey eyes that no longer seemed cool or remote, the hard yet somehow sensual line of his mouth, the tiny lines that only showed when he frowned or smiled. So many small yet important details that she seemed to be seeing for the very first time.

Lacey was briefly shaken out of her reverie by someone accidentally jostling her. As she stumbled off balance, Marcus automatically shot one hand out to steady her. His fingers closed over her wrist, then seemed to grip it for much longer than was necessary.

It was the first time he had ever touched her. In the office she had always been scrupulously careful to avoid any physical contact, she couldn't remember even brushing against him by accident. Now the sensation of those warm, strong fingers against her skin made her actually begin to shake, she was totally confused by what was happening to her. The whole world seemed to be turning into an unreal place, only the man standing opposite her was still made of solid flesh and blood. Even the people all around her had somehow faded into shadows, they didn't seem really to exist. Reality had narrowed down to the couple of square feet of ground on which the two of them were standing, by a holy river in a strange land.

Seconds later, Marcus abruptly released her wrist, and as he let go of her she heard him give a small growl of irritation.

'I don't want this. I don't *need* it.'

Lacey absently rubbed her arm, which seemed to be both aching and tingling where he had gripped it. She didn't know what to say, how to react, and in the end she gave a rather nervous laugh. 'I know that the sunrise is meant to be a special, rather magic time, but don't you think this is overdoing it a bit?'

Marcus swung round and fixed his gaze on her warningly. 'Don't joke about this, Lacey. I don't find it in the least bit funny.'

Nor did she, as a matter of fact. It was only her over-stretched nerves that had made her laugh like that. But on the other hand, she didn't really understand it, either.

'Perhaps we ought to talk about it,' she suggested, looking at him edgily.

'It's certainly something that we've got to get straightened out,' he agreed tightly. 'But not here. Back at the hotel.'

She had no intention of arguing with him about that. There was something about this place that seemed to turn everything topsy-turvy, she wasn't anxious to stay here one moment longer than she had to. Something very odd had happened at that moment when the sun had risen and touched them with its golden light. And the spell hadn't quite let go of her yet, she could feel it still tugging at her, sending silent tremors through her raw nerve-ends.

Marcus swung round and set off at a fast pace, back up the steps of the ghat. He didn't even look round to see if she was following him. She was, though, stumbling along in his wake, still a little mystified—and unnerved—by what had happened to them at the water's edge.

In just minutes, they had left the river behind; the bustle, the noise and the smell of the city began to close around them again, and the last of the magic finally dissolved away. It didn't take them long to reach the hotel. Marcus led her straight to her room, then followed her in. He didn't say anything immediately, though; instead he prowled restlessly over to the far side of the room. Lacey watched him with troubled eyes. This might have been easier to cope with if he had *looked* the same as usual, in a dark suit, immaculate shirt and silk tie. It was the image she had got used to over the past year, the well dressed, efficient businessman. This morning, though, like most mornings since their arrival in India, he was wearing denim jeans and a white cotton shirt, and the casual clothes somehow made him look younger, more approachable, less formidable.

But then he swung round to face her, and she recognised the expression on his face only too well, she had seen it dozens of times in the office when something had happened that hadn't pleased him. And it was becoming increasingly obvious that what had happened between them down at that landing stage hadn't been to his liking one little bit.

'All right,' he said abruptly. 'I suppose we might as well get this out into the open. It wasn't something that I ever expected to happen, but now it has we had better find some way of dealing with it.'

Lacey looked at him guardedly. 'To be perfectly honest, I'm not sure that I know what you're talking about. Oh, I realise something a bit odd happened down at that landing stage, but I really don't understand what it was. Do you? If you do, perhaps you'd better explain it to me.'

He stared at her in pure disbelief. 'Come on Lacey, no one can be *that* naïve. You're certainly old enough to recognise sexual attraction when it jumps up and hits you round the face.'

A hot surge of colour instantly flooded her skin. 'S-sexual attraction?' she stuttered, her breathing becoming slightly strangled. 'But that's impossible! You've got to be joking——'

'I told you before, I don't joke about things like that,' he reminded her rather grimly.

'But——' Words failed Lacey, she couldn't think of a single thing to say. Anyway, she wasn't sure that she even believed him. How on earth could they be sexually attracted to each other? The whole idea was totally crazy.

Marcus was glaring at her now in fierce frustration. In fact, he looked as if he rather badly wanted to shake her. She even saw him lift his hands. Then he lowered them again, and she guessed that he had decided it definitely wouldn't be a good idea to touch her. After all, look what had happened the last time.

'When I was planning this trip, it never occurred to me that anything like this would happen,' he growled, running his fingers broodingly through the gold silk of his hair. 'It probably *wouldn't* have happened if it hadn't been for that damned sunrise. It seemed to make everything look different—it made *you* look different.'

But Lacey was hardly listening to what he was saying now, she was still rather frantically trying to sort it all out inside her own head. Was there the slightest possibility he was right? Was it really a strong physical response that had suddenly surged up from nowhere and blazed between them? It was a pretty hard explanation to swallow, but she had to admit she was hardly an authority on the subject, while she was sure Marcus Caradin had enough experience for half a dozen men. If he was adamant that was what it was, she supposed she would just have to accept it and somehow come to terms with it.

She lifted her shoulders in a rather helpless shrug. 'I'm sorry. I don't know how it could have happened——'

'Don't apologise!' he cut in irritably. 'It's not your fault. It's not anybody's fault, although it *is* a bloody nuisance. I suppose the most practical way of dealing with it is to send you straight back to England. At least that'll stop it going any further.'

At that, her eyes instantly took on an ominous gleam. 'You seem to be automatically assuming that I want it to go further,' she responded sharply. 'Well, I don't! As far as I'm concerned, I just want to forget all about it.'

And she wasn't lying, either. There was no way she wanted to get sexually entangled with Marcus Caradin. Or with anyone, come to that. She might not have had a lot of personal experience but she certainly wasn't ignorant, she had seen the deep devastation that casual affairs could cause. If it was some kind of sexual awareness that had flared into life between them this morning, then she definitely didn't want anything to do with it.

Marcus was studying her assessingly now, as if trying to gauge if she was telling the truth. Really, she thought to herself with a swift surge of anger, he wasn't *that* irresistible. Did he think she was going to lose all control and fling herself straight into his arms?

Apparently not, as his next words confirmed.

'All right, let's look at this whole thing from a purely practical point of view,' he said with sudden decisiveness. 'You're a sensible, level-headed girl, Lacey. We've never had any problems working together in the past, and as long as we're careful, we shouldn't have any difficulties in the future. What happened this morning was almost certainly a fluke, an unfortunate combination of atmosphere and a rather odd set of circumstances. There's no reason why it should ever happen again. So— shall we agree to put the whole thing behind us, forget it ever happened and get on with the job we came here to do?'

'That suits me fine,' she nodded immediately.

Marcus glanced at his watch. 'Then let's make a start right now. We'll meet downstairs in half an hour—that'll give you time to have breakfast—and we'll begin doing the rounds of the local hotels. Then after lunch, I've an appointment with one of the local coach operators. I want to get everything settled today so that we can start out for Kathmandu in the morning.' He paused, and she had the impression that there was something else he wanted to say. But then his grey eyes reverted to their customary coolness and, without another word, he left the room.

Lacey stood exactly where she was for a couple more minutes. She still felt turned upside down by what had happened, she was having trouble convincing herself that she hadn't just woken up from a rather exotic although disturbing dream.

Then her hand drifted up to her hair, she touched the petals of the marigold that Marcus had slid into the dark red strands. Very slowly, she pulled out the flower and stared at it for several seconds. No, it hadn't been a dream. Although perhaps it would have been better if it had been.

She gave a faint sigh, then tossed the flower to one side. Sensible girls didn't wear marigolds in their hair. Sensible girls worked hard, and kept their feet very firmly on the ground. And she was determined to remain a sensible girl, no matter what happened.

* * *

She found she wasn't particularly looking forward to seeing Marcus again. It was all very well for them to agree that they would just forget about what had happened and go straight back to their old, formal working relationship. She couldn't help feeling that actually doing it might be a little harder than either of them had anticipated.

The breakfast she gulped down gave her nervous indigestion, and when she saw Marcus coming over to meet her, her skin immediately broke out in a rash of goose-pimples. Get a hold on yourself, Lacey, she told herself, slightly panic-stricken. It's only your boss, the man you've worked for all year without any problems. And don't forget, you don't go for his type, he's the last man on earth you'd ever want to get involved with.

It soon became clear that Marcus wasn't having any difficulty in dealing with the situation. His manner was brisk and businesslike, his voice crisp and without the slightest trace of any warmth, any intimacy. Taking her cue from him, Lacey responded with equal detachment, and firmly ignored the faint fluttering in the pit of her stomach as she followed him out of the hotel.

A couple of hours later, her feet were throbbing and her head was aching. Although Marcus was all cool efficiency on the outside, she had soon discovered he was actually in a very odd sort of mood, short-tempered and brooding, ready to find fault with just about everything. They had already toured half a dozen hotels, but he had rejected every one of them out of hand. It looked as if it was going to be absolutely impossible to please him today.

'This one looks ideal,' she told him firmly, as they returned to the lobby after an extensive tour of yet another of Varanasi's hotels. 'The dining-room's fine, they offer a good, varied menu, the kitchen's clean and well equipped, the bedrooms are beautifully furnished and they've even got en suite bathrooms. What else could you possibly want?'

'The air-conditioning isn't quite right,' he replied, with a dark frown.

Lacey let out a frustrated sigh. Her legs were aching so badly they felt as if they wanted to fold up under her, and her headache was getting steadily worse. What was more, she knew perfectly well that this hotel was entirely suitable in every way. The only trouble was, Marcus wouldn't admit it. In fact, in the mood he was in right now, there probably wasn't a hotel in the whole of India that he would be willing to pronounce as satisfactory.

She stared up at him with more than a touch of exasperation. 'Look, the people who are going to book this holiday aren't going to expect luxury accommodation. After all, that's why most of them come on this kind of holiday, isn't it? Because they're tired of five-star hotels and endless days spent lounging around a swimming-pool? All they're going to want at night is a decent meal and a comfortable bed, and this hotel can definitely provide both those things.'

Marcus frowned again, and Lacey's mouth drooped, she felt sure he was going to veto this hotel, the way he had vetoed all the others. Then, to her surprise—and relief—he eventually gave a curt nod.

'You're probably right. Let's go and discuss terms with the manager.'

But Lacey briefly closed her aching eyes. Quite suddenly she couldn't face another session of haggling over prices.

'Would you mind if I waited outside? I've got a

splitting headache, I really need some fresh air.'

A flash of impatience instantly revealed itself in
Marcus's eyes. Lacey saw it, and silently groaned. The
man had no feelings at all—and the trouble was, he
didn't expect other people to have any, either. She could
collapse at his feet, and his only reaction would be one of
annoyance because she wasn't available to take notes.

Then she was surprised to see his features change,
softening just a fraction. 'I suppose I have been pushing
you rather hard,' he conceded. 'Do you want to go back to
the hotel and rest?'

Slightly astonished by his sudden change of attitude,
she shook her head. 'No, I'll be fine once I've taken a
couple of aspirins and got some fresh air.'

'You're sure? I can easily deal with the rest of the day's
schedule on my own.'

Much more of this concern and she would start feeling
faint with shock, she told herself with unaccustomed
cynicism. Anyway, wouldn't it be better to take him up
on his offer? She had a suspicion that her headache and
his tendency to find fault with everything were both
caused by the same thing, the fact that they weren't
entirely at ease with each other this morning, not after
that odd episode by the river's edge. Perhaps it would be
better if they had a few hours apart, to give themselves a
chance to sort things out and somehow get back to
normal.

Then she lifted her head with fresh determination.
There was nothing to sort out! she told herself firmly.
They had just both got a little carried away with the
exotic atmosphere; the mystic east had played a trick on
them, getting under their skin without their realising it.
There was no chance of its happening again, though,
they would both be on their guard against it in the future,

so there was no reason why they shouldn't carry on working together as if nothing had happened.

'I'll be all right,' she assured him sturdily. 'I'll wait for you by the hotel entrance.'

She made her way to the ladies' cloakroom, washed down a couple of aspirins with a glass of water, then left the hotel. A couple of minutes later, she was grimacing slightly. She had told Marcus that she needed some fresh air, but in India the air never seemed to be particularly fresh, not in the centre of town, anyway. Instead, it carried traces of a hundred and one pungent smells, and the noise all around her was pretty ear-splitting too, bells and horns blaring out, street-traders yelling at the tops of their voices, and the constant jabber of conversations in languages that were totally foreign to her.

Her headache was beginning to ease a little, though, the aspirins were already taking effect, and after a while she wandered down a narrow alley opposite the hotel. The tiny shops that lined it were crammed invitingly with billowing silks in rainbow colours, copper and brass ornaments, silver jewellery, exquisite carpets and exotic-looking food. Somehow—she wasn't quite sure how—she ended up buying a small statue of a Buddha, painted in bright, garish colours and studded with glass beads. As she headed back to the hotel, she stared at it a little ruefully. Perhaps she could give it to Jane; her flat-mate had a taste for the unusual.

Marcus was already waiting for her by the hotel entrance. In fact, he wasn't just waiting, he was glancing around with an expression on his face that looked remarkably like acute anxiety. When he caught sight of her, a swift flicker of relief briefly showed in his eyes.

'Did you think I'd managed to get lost?' Lacey asked cheerfully.

'That's not particularly amusing,' he responded with unexpected sharpness. Then he seemed to realise he was over-reacting, made an obvious effort to relax, and instead fixed his gaze on the Buddha she was holding. 'What on earth have you got there?'

'I'm not sure,' she admitted. 'I sort of bought it by mistake.'

One straight eyebrow lifted expressively. 'I should think "a mistake" describes that statue very well. Who are you planning on giving it to?' He paused for a fraction of a second. 'A boyfriend?' he added, his voice somehow sounding just a shade too casual.

'It's so awful that I probably won't have the nerve to give it to anyone,' she answered, rather evasively. She certainly wouldn't have the nerve to give it to Robert, she told herself with a faint grin. His flat was furnished with exquisite taste, the only ornaments were fine porcelain and antique silver. She could just imagine the pained expression that would appear on his face if she presented him with this primitive little Buddha, painted in bright primary colours and plastered with cheap glass beads. Anyway, she had a funny feeling that she wouldn't be seeing Robert again. Being this far away from him was somehow making her see their relationship in a new light, she was beginning to realise just how empty it was. Not that she thought he would be particularly upset by a clean break between them. Theirs had certainly never been a grand passionate affair, they had been more like a sedate, middle-aged couple who went out together simply for companionship.

Coming out of her introspective thoughts, she glanced up at Marcus and discovered that his grey gaze was now locked on to her with piercing intensity. For some reason, she found that hard scrutiny distinctly unnerv-

ing, and she shuffled her feet a little uneasily. As if he
suddenly realised that he had been staring at her, his
features instantly switched back to their usual cool,
unreadable expression.

'We'll have a quick lunch, then go and visit a couple of
the local coach operators,' he told her rather abruptly. 'Is
your headache better now?' he added, almost as an
afterthought. 'Can you cope with the afternoon's
itinerary?'

'I feel fine,' she replied, but it wasn't strictly true. Her
headache had gone, but she couldn't quite get rid of the
niggling sense of apprehension that had been lurking in
the pit of her stomach all morning. Just ignore it, she told
herself firmly. It's not important, it'll be gone by
tomorrow.

They followed an exhausting schedule for the rest of
the afternoon, and by evening she felt totally drained, she
just wanted to collapse into bed and sleep for at least
twenty-four hours. Not that there was much chance of
that, she reminded herself ruefully. Marcus would be up
at the crack of dawn tomorrow, ready to put in another
punishing day's work.

She went up to her room, showered, then wandered
over to the window. She stood there for a long time, just
silently staring out. The sights and sounds of the river
washed over her, she could see barge lights twinkling,
could hear the light gurgling of lapping water. And
overhead, a huge moon gleamed palely in the dark velvet
sky.

Without any warning, vivid memories abruptly
washed back over her, for a few moments she found
herself unwillingly reliving those strange moments when
she and Marcus had faced each other by the river's edge,
both of them bathed in the pale glow of the rising sun.

Then she remembered the touch of his fingers against her bare skin, and she shivered deeply.

'Come on, Lacey, don't make more of it than it actually was,' she lectured herself rather shakily. 'It was just a touch of the old eastern magic, that's all. Forget about it—you've *got* to forget about it.'

She swung round, deliberately turning her back on the seductive scene from the window, climbed into bed and determinedly closed her eyes. And much to her relief, she almost immediately drifted into a deep and dreamless sleep.

CHAPTER THREE

WHEN she tottered down to breakfast the following morning, still only half awake, she found Marcus already sitting at their table. That very quickly woke her up. As she sat down opposite him, their eyes briefly met, and she was the first to look away, busying herself with her napkin.

'I've already ordered for both of us,' Marcus informed her. 'I want to make an early start today.'

Lacey groaned inwardly. Hadn't he ever heard of a rest day? 'You mean we're leaving for Kathmandu?' she said, with a distinct lack of enthusiasm.

'As soon as we've finished breakfast. There's nothing more to do here in Varanasi. I've made the provisional hotel bookings, and come to an arrangement with one of the local coach operators, who's willing to supply all the transport we're likely to need. There's no point in staying here any longer.' He paused, looking at her thoughtfully. 'Tell me, Lacey,' he went on, 'if you were one of our customers, booked on this holiday, would you prefer to travel on to Kathmandu by private coach or by local transport?'

'I'd definitely prefer to go by luxury, air-conditioned coach,' she told him bluntly. 'I know that a lot of people think that local transport's quaint and colourful, but in my opinion it's just slow, dusty and uncomfortable. Like that train journey from Delhi to Varanasi,' she added, with a deep grimace at the memory.

Marcus's eyes lightened with an unexpected touch of

amusement. 'Where's your sense of adventure?' he mocked gently. 'I thought girls of your age always wanted to travel, to see as much of the world as they could.'

Lacey scowled. 'I've already seen far more of the world than I want to, thank you very much.'

He began to look interested. 'How come?'

Too late, she realised she had said rather more than she had intended. 'My mother's always travelled a great deal,' she admitted at last, with some reluctance. 'Until a couple of years ago, I always went with her. America, Europe—even Australia—although we never stayed in any one place for very long.'

Marcus leant forward slightly. 'What about your father?' he asked. 'Did he travel with you?'

'He died when I was very young. I can't even remember him, at least I don't think I can. Sometimes I get these vague memories of someone tall and very dark, but I might be just making that up from the old photos I've seen of him.'

Marcus's gaze drifted to the bright blaze of her hair. 'Then you get your colourings from your mother?'

'Oh, no, she's dark as well——' Lacey began, then she very hurriedly shut up. That was something she didn't even want to think about, let alone discuss with Marcus Caradin. She had long ago reached her own private conclusions about the whole touchy subject. After all, what were the odds on two dark-haired, dark-eyed parents producing a red-haired, green-eyed child? And considering her mother's track record, there was no reason to believe that she had been any more content with just one man during her marriage than she had been during all the long years since.

'Did your mother remarry?' asked Marcus, after a thoughtful pause.

'Yes. A couple of times.' Then she realised that she hadn't meant to tell him that, either. What was the matter with her tongue this morning? It kept running away with her, letting slip a lot of information that she would have much preferred to keep private.

One gold eyebrow lifted expressively. 'If she's managed to snare three husbands, she must have quite a lot going for her. Is she very beautiful?'

That seemed a fairly harmless question, so Lacey answered it without too many qualms. 'I don't know—yes, I suppose she is.' When Marcus looked at her a little quizzically, she went on, 'Quite honestly, you don't notice her looks. She's got—well, to use a rather hackneyed old phrase, I suppose you'd say she's got sex appeal. Whenever she walks into a room, every male who isn't either senile or short-sighted can't take his eyes off her. Do you know what I mean?'

For a moment, a rather disturbing glint appeared in Marcus's eyes. 'Oh, yes,' he said softly, 'I know exactly what you mean.'

A little uneasily, Lacey chattered on. 'She's in her forties now, but she's still slaying them in their droves. She can't settle, you see, she's like a butterfly, always flitting here, flitting there. And she can't *help* it if men fall in love with her.'

'You rush to her defence very quickly,' Marcus commented. 'You don't resent her for not giving you a more—conventional, settled childhood?' he finished, with unexpected tactfulness.

'Of course not,' Lacey answered, without hesitation. 'Oh sure, there've been times when she's driven me mad, and I knew I didn't want her kind of life, I wanted to settle somewhere and put down roots, but I always loved her. I still do. It's just—well, we reached the stage where we couldn't really live together any longer.' And she definitely wasn't going to tell him about that, the emotional scenes, the final painful break-up. Anyway, it was all in the past now, it was pointless to dig it up again.

The waiter brought their breakfast at that point, and she thankfully seized on the opportunity to stop talking about herself. Keeping her head down, she concentrated on her food, although she was beginning to wish she could have eaten breakfast alone. Marcus Caradin was definitely beginning to have an adverse effect on her digestive system, her appetite kept threatening to pack up completely whenever he was around.

Much to her relief, he didn't try to probe any further into her personal affairs. Instead, he poured himself another cup of coffee, then stared into the distance, as if he were thinking something over. 'We'll travel to Kathmandu by local transport,' he announced decisively, a few minutes later. Ignoring Lacey's grimace of dismay, he went on, 'Our clients always seem to enjoy travelling on local buses whenever they get the chance, so we'll try this route ourselves, and see how it works out. If it turns out to be too gruelling, then we'll hire a private coach for this part of the journey once the regular package tours get under way.'

Lacey gave a silent groan. 'All the way to Kathmandu by local bus?' she echoed, with a clear lack of enthusiasm.

'Consider yourself lucky,' he told her coolly. 'In a few months, people are going to be paying Caradin Tours hundreds of pounds for the privilege of going on this trip—and you're getting it for free. Have you finished breakfast?' She nodded. In fact, she was beginning to wish she hadn't eaten anything at all. 'Then you'd better go and get packed. We'll be leaving in half an hour. '

'Only a masochist would book a holiday with Caradin Tours,' she grumbled under her breath as she followed him out of the dining-room.

And she was beginning to think that only a masochist would willingly work for Marcus Caradin. When she got back to England, she was very seriously going to consider giving in her notice. She glared at his broad back, then trudged upstairs to pack.

The bus journey to Kathmandu turned out to be even worse than she had expected. By the first night, they had only reached the border town of Raxaul, where immigration and customs officers checked and stamped their passports, made a desultory search of their luggage, then welcomed them to Nepal.

After a night in a local hotel, they set off early the next morning in search of the bus which would take them on the last leg of their journey. Lacey didn't feel in the least thrilled that they were at last in Nepal. All she wanted was to reach Kathmandu, check into a decent hotel, then leap straight into a hot bath and stay there until all the hundreds of separate aches had soaked their way out of her poor jolted body.

Even Marcus looked distinctly taken aback when they finally found the bus that would take them to Kathmandu. Several of the windows were missing, a couple of the tyres looked frighteningly bald, and Lacey had the impression that only thick layers of the rust were holding the ageing bodywork together.

'It's such *fun* to travel by local tranpsort,' she remarked with heavy sarcasm. 'Wondering if it's going to break down, fall apart, tip you straight into the nearest ravine—I mean, it all adds to the sense of adventure, don't you think?'

Marcus shot her a look which warned her that it definitely wouldn't be wise to make any more remarks along the same lines. Muttering darkly under her breath, she hauled her suitcase up on to the roof, where it joined a mound of sacks, a pile of spare wheels, and a crate of chickens. Then she and Marcus found a seat inside, along with the rest of the passengers, who seemed to be a mixture of Hindus, Nepalese, and a handful of weary, dusty tourists of several nationalities.

As the bus chugged its way noisily along, though, even Lacey was impressed by her first glimpses of the Himalayas. Capped with glittering white ice, ringed with thin collars of cloud, they soared so high into the sky that their presence was quite awesome. For a while, she even forgot about her tired, aching body.

The bus trundled on across a high plain, where rice and maize grew on every available square foot of land, and small figures steered ox-drawn ploughs, scythed corn or theshed grain. Then it roared down into a gorge, and all that could be seen for a while was high vertical cliff walls.

Lacey turned to Marcus. 'You haven't said a word since we left Raxaul.'

'That's probably because I've been too busy praying,' he replied drily. 'If everyone on this bus sends up a plea to whatever deity they worship, perhaps one of them will step in and get us to Kathmandu in one piece.'

She glanced around at the other passengers. 'They all seem to be taking the whole thing fairly calmly,' she remarked. 'Perhaps the bus is in better condition that it looks.'

'And perhaps the hole in the floor by my left foot is just a figment of my imagination.'

She took a quick glance, then hurriedly looked away

again and swallowed hard.

'Well, no one else seems very worried,' she said, trying hard to sound optimistic.

'That's probably because they have a rather different outlook on things from ours. The famous eastern fatalism—what will be will be, and all that.'

'And that's not your way of looking at things?' she guessed without too much difficulty.

'Definitely not,' Marcus agreed, without hesitation. 'I like to carve out my own future, run my life the way I want it to be, the way which best suits me.'

'And do things always work out the way you want them to?'

He paused briefly. 'No, not always,' he finally admitted, rather curtly.

Lacey was quiet for a couple of minutes, then she turned back to him again. 'What did you do before you bought out Worldwide Travel and turned it into Caradin Tours?'

'Why do you want to know?' he countered, a closed expression crossing his face, as if he didn't particularly like the way the conversation was going.

She shrugged. 'No particular reason. It's just that no one knows very much about you. You arrived like a bolt from the blue one morning, turned the entire company upside down, gradually turned a huge loss into a financial profit, and I don't think anyone's quite figured out yet how you did it.'

'Hard work, and a good basic knowledge of the travel industry,' he said succinctly. 'It's as simple as that.'

Lacey raised one eyebrow sceptically. 'If it's that easy, why aren't we all business tycoons?'

Again, there was that brief pause, 'Probably because few people are prepared to put in the sheer hard work it requires,' he replied finally. 'It takes up virtually your entire life, there's no time for leisure, for relaxation, for personal involvements, and most people aren't willing to give those up.'

'But you were?'

'It rather looks like it, doesn't it?'

Something in his tone clearly warned her he didn't want to pursue that particular line of questioning. And remembering the rumours about a messy divorce, realising that he might have very personal reasons for wanting to immerse himself in hard work, she quickly abandoned the subject. Touchy about her own private life and background, she was quick to appreciate that others might be equally reluctant to reveal the rattling skeletons that lurked in just about everyone's cupboard.

All the same, her curiosity wasn't satisfied yet, and she didn't see any reason why she shouldn't go back to her earlier question, which he hadn't answered.

'Well, what *did* you do before you set up Caradin Tours?'

He shrugged. 'I've always been involved with the travel business, one way or another. I started out as a courier, travelling all over Europe with different groups of tourists. Then I got a chance to buy out a small local travel company that had got itself into financial difficulties. I gradually built it up in the same way I'm building up Caradin Tours, by offering holidays to places that were off the beaten track. While I'd been working as a courier, I'd spent most of my free time exploring the less well known parts of Europe. When people came in wanting holidays away from the popular, overcrowded resorts, I knew exactly where to send them. Word got around, and that side of the business began to expand at a fairly phenomenal rate.'

'Where did you get the capital to buy the travel company in the first place?' Lacey asked curiously. 'Couriers aren't *that* well paid.'

He shot a quizzical look at her. 'You're not shy about asking personal questions, are you?'

She flushed slightly. 'You don't have to answer them, if you don't want to,' she replied a little defensively.

Much to her surprise, he gave a faint smile and then relaxed back in his seat. 'It's no great secret,' he said, a moment later. 'I had a small amount of capital of my own, and I managed to swing a fairly hefty bank loan to make up the difference.'

'What happened to the company?'

'What do you mean?'

'Why aren't you still running it?' Lacey asked.

A brief frown darkened his face. 'A couple of years ago, I sold out.' Quickly forestalling her next question, he added, 'I don't intend to go into the whys and wherefores. Afterwards, I travelled abroad for a few months, but then I realised I needed to work again, so I came back and set up Caradin Tours. It was touch and go for a while at the beginning, I was rather short of working capital, but everything seems to be running smoothly now, and there's no reason why we shouldn't keep expanding over the next couple of years.'

'And do you really think just anyone could have accomplished all that?' she said, unable to keep a note of admiration out of her voice.

'With hard work and a strong sense of commitment, there's absolutely no reason why not,' Marcus said firmly.

'Hmm,' she snorted, totally unconvinced. 'You'd be hard pushed to find anyone at Caradin Tours who'd agree with you about that. Do you know what they call you behind your back?'

'Is it repeatable?' Marcus enquired drily.

'Not only that, but it's actually a compliment,' she assured him cheerfully. 'They've nicknamed you "Miracle Man". Everyone knows what a financial mess the company was in, they reckon it's little short of a miracle that you've turned the company round in such a short time, that it's actually producing a profit just a year after you took over.'

'A very small profit,' he pointed out.

'But it'll be much bigger next year. And after that— who knows?'

The bus hit a particularly bumpy patch of road at that point, which effectively put a stop to all conversation. Lacey clutched nervously at the edge of her seat and hoped her stomach was up to all the jolting, then she gave a sigh of relief and relaxed slightly as the road straightened out again. A couple of minutes later, she stifled a yawn, then another. She hadn't slept particularly well at the hotel in Raxaul last night, and she was getting more and more sleepy. Perhaps she could snatch a quick nap, it would be quite a while yet before they reached Kathmandu. Glancing at Marcus, she found he had pulled a guide-book from his pocket and was flicking through the pages, not paying any attention to her now. She slid further down into her seat, closed her heavy eyes, and soon drifted into a light sleep.

When she eventually woke up again, she felt so warm and comfortable that she didn't want to move. Rubbing her eyes dozily, she gave a small sigh of pure contentment and was sorely tempted to go straight back to sleep.

Then it slowly dawned on her *why* she was so warm and comfortable. She was curled snugly up against Marcus, her head on his shoulder, her body sagging against his in a state of blissful relaxation.

Suddenly completely awake, she shot bolt upright and felt a hot surge of colour sweep over her face. 'Sorry,' she muttered in a strangled tone.

'It's all right,' Marcus replied casually. Yet she knew perfectly well that it wasn't all right, she had felt the tautness of his muscles during those few seconds before she had jerked away from him.

Embarrassment and confusion still flooding through her, she turned her head away and stared out of the window. 'Where are we?'

'We've just reached Kathmandu.' His voice definitely sounded strained, but there wasn't time to worry about it because the bus had begun to grind to a halt, and the rest of the passengers were getting ready to pour off.

She got stiffly to her feet and followed them off the bus, then waited until Marcus had retrieved their luggage. Looking around, she found she was standing in the centre of a square, surrounded by shops, market-stalls, tea-houses and temples. As at Varanasi, the air was drenched with a mixture of scents, some exotic like incense and spices, others definitely a lot less pleasant. The skyline seemed littered with the pagoda roofs of yet more temples, while in the distance shimmered the foothills of the Himalayas.

'Kathmandu seems to be knee-deep in temples,' Lacey commented as Marcus rejoined her, carrying their luggage.

'It's reckoned to have more temples than any other city in the world,' Marcus answered. She was relieved to find he sounded quite relaxed again now, and told herself she had probably just imagined the tension in him before. 'The Nepalese are mostly either Buddhists or Hindus,' he went on, 'but they share their places of worship quite

happily with each other, there aren't any great religious
divisions here as there are in so many other parts of the
world.'

But Lacey had already begun to lose interest. She was
sure it was all absolutely fascinating, but right now she
just couldn't seem to dredge up any enthusiasm.
Travelling around, arriving in new places, had long ago
lost the power to enchant her; there had been too many
new places, new people, all whizzing in and out of her life
through all the years she had been growing up. She would
just get used to a particular house, a particular town, a
particular country, when her mother would sweep in and
announce they were moving again. And Lacey would
know perfectly well what that meant. Her mother had
just met someone new, she was about to launch into yet
another short-lived but turbulent affair, dragging Lacey
unwillingly along in her wake——

'Day-dreaming?' enquired Marcus quietly.

Lacey jumped slightly. She hadn't realised he had been
watching her with unexpected intensity. For a moment,
she felt herself stiffen. How her mother would have loved
Marcus Caradin! He was precisely the type of man she
always went for, strong, intelligent, someone who carried
with him that invisible aura of power and authority—
and the silent but unmistakable promise of sexual skill
and expertise.

Suddenly flustered, and frightened that he would see
her face, be able to guess what she was thinking, she bent
down and began to fumble with her suitcase. 'Let's find a
hotel,' she said in a rather taut voice. 'I want a hot meal, a
hot bath, and an early night.'

Marcus's eyes narrowed slightly. 'You really do hate
travelling, don't you?' he said, with a small frown.

'It's not my favourite past-time,' she agreed. 'But don't

worry, I'm not about to give in my notice and walk out on you. Although I might if you've got any more two-day bus journeys in mind,' she warned darkly. 'I ache in places you wouldn't believe!'

It didn't take them long to find a suitable hotel, and after a soak in the tub and a change of clothes, Lacey felt in a rather more relaxed frame of mind. She brushed her bright red hair, leaving it lying loose around her shoulders, dabbed on a little make-up, then made her way down to the dining-room.

Marcus was already there, waiting for her. As she sat down at the table, he glanced up at her, and as those familiar grey eyes fixed briefly on to hers, she experienced the all-too-familiar sensation of her appetite flying right out of the window.

This was ridiculous! she lectured herself silently. If she didn't put a stop to this right now, she would be as thin as a rake by the time they finally got back to England.

When the first course arrived, she stubbornly forced herself to eat. She found she could just about manage to swallow a few mouthfuls if she kept her gaze fixed very firmly on her plate, and didn't let herself look up at the man sitting opposite her. She did notice, though, that Marcus didn't seem particularly hungry either, although he refilled his wine glass several times.

He eventually pushed his half-full plate away, and glanced around with obvious restlessness.

'I think I'll take a walk around the city,' he said eventually in an abrupt voice. Then he added, with clear reluctance, 'Do you want to come along?'

Lacey knew perfectly well that she ought to say no, but quite suddenly the thought of sitting alone in the hotel wasn't in the least appealing; in fact she found it distinctly depressing. Anyway, what harm could there be in a short stroll through the crowded streets of Kathmandu? And she was still stiff from sitting on that bus for all those hours, some exercise might help to straighten the kinks out of her muscles.

A few minutes later, they left the hotel. It was dusk now, and in the half-light the city had taken on a more mysterious atmosphere, although the air was no less pungent, and it certainly wasn't any quieter. Nepalese music drifted out from the tea-houses, mixing with the more familiar pop music blaring out from radios and cassette players, taxi horns and bicycle bells set up a minor cacophony of their own, and there was the constant jabber of voices as people haggled over the price of whatever they wanted to buy from the ever-present street-traders.

Lacey pointed to a small group of Nepalese who were stopping in front of an elaborately decorated canopy which had a small statue underneath it.

'What are they doing?' she asked.

'They're making an offering to the Lord Indra, the ruler of Heaven,' Marcus explained. 'We've arrived at the start of the festival of Indra Jatra. During the festival a young girl called the Kumari, who's widely regarded as a living goddess, will paint a symbolic red mark on the forehead of the King of Nepal. That will give him the right to rule for another year. Then the young girl—the Kumari—will be drawn round the streets of Kathmandu in a chariot.'

'How do they choose who's to be the Kumari?' asked Lacey, with growing interest.

'She has to be a Buddhist, and to belong to the caste of goldsmiths,' Marcus told her. 'And among other things, she has to have perfect skin and not have lost any teeth.'

'That sounds like a fairly tall order.'

'She can only be the Kumari until she reaches adolescence,' continued Marcus. 'As soon as she begins menstruation, she has to be immediately replaced by another young girl.'

'What happens to her once she's stopped being the Kumari?' asked Lacey curiously.

'She goes back to living an ordinary life again.'

'That must be rather difficult when you've spent most of your life being a living goddess,' she commented.

'And there are one or two other problems, as well,' warned Marcus with a slight twitch of his mouth.

'Such as what?'

'You have to be a fairly brave man to marry an ex-Kumari. It's widely believed that the man who takes her virginity will die shortly afterwards.'

Lacey's eyebrows shot up. 'And *does* he?'

Marcus grinned. 'The last girl who was the Kumari is happily married, and her husband's alive and in good health.'

'That's just as well,' she told him with an answering grin. 'If a rumour like that ever took hold and started to spread, it could have fairly drastic consequences. Oh, look!' They had reached the main square now, and her attention had been diverted from the fate of the Kumari by the sight of the temples lit by thousands of small oil lamps.

There were far more people here, she and Marcus were starting to be jostled by the crowd, they kept being pushed closer and closer together. Finally finding themselves hemmed in on all sides, they were forced to stop along with everyone else, to watch some exotically masked dancers who were whirling and leaping themselves almost into a frenzy. As the crowd of people pushed forward, all of them trying to get a better look,

she could feel Marcus's arm, his hip, his upper thigh
pressed hard against her, they were locked close together
by the pressure of the bodies all around them, they
couldn't escape from the enforced and unexpectedly
intimate contact.

She heard Marcus give a small growl of irritation.

'There are too many people here,' he muttered rather
abruptly. 'Let's go somewhere a bit quieter.'

He turned and physically forced his way back through
the crowd, leaving her to struggle along in his wake, only
managing to keep track of him because his bright gold
hair gleamed like a beacon in the darkness. Then he
suddenly disappeared from sight altogether, she found
herself surrounded by total strangers who suddenly
seemed to be crushing her, smothering her, and for a few
moments she felt a wave of pure panic roll over her.

Then cool, strong fingers closed over her own, and she
sagged with relief as she instinctively recognised Marcus's touch. He towed her easily through the crowds until
they finally reached a dimly lit corner in one of the
temples. There were far fewer people here, and she began
to breathe easily again.

'I don't like large crowds,' she confessed, with a
grimace. 'They always make me feel as if I'm
suffocating.'

'Are you all right now? Do you want to go back to the
hotel?'

'No, I'm OK. Let's take a look round the temples——'

Her voice trailed away as she realised he was still
holding her hand, his fingers linked lightly through her
own, their grip warm and firm. She swallowed hard and
suddenly felt a little unsteady on her feet. Her palm
seemed to fit so perfectly against his, it might almost
have been made to measure. For a few heady moments,

she found herself wondering if the rest of their bodies would fit together with such perfection. Then her head shot up, she was totally horrified by the thoughts that had started to rush through her confused head.

Almost as if reading her mind, Marcus quickly let go of her, and she felt her pulse gradually begin to slow down a little. All the same, she still felt highly disturbed, and she hurriedly moved a safe distance away from him, then made a pretence of being very interested in an exquisitely carved door panel.

When she finally turned back to him, she had herself more or less under control again. Then she saw that Marcus was staring at her with a dark, almost brooding intensity, and her nerve-ends started to quiver all over again, and there was a slightly frantic fluttering somewhere deep in the pit of her stomach. Swallowing hard, she took a couple more steps away from him, then she gazed fixedly at the panels of decorative carvings that covered the temple walls; the carvings were vivid and lifelike, gods and godesses, birds and snakes, and——

'Oh!' Lacey gulped hard, and briefly forgot the turmoil that Marcus had started to stir up inside her. To her annoyance, she found she had actually started to blush. A nearby oil-lamp was making this particular group of carvings stand out in high relief, and they could only be described as rather outrageously erotic.

Marcus moved a litle closer, and Lacey felt her skin begin to prickle warningly.

'Do they shock you?' he asked in an even voice.

'No, I don't think so,' she answered, her gaze sliding back to the carvings. 'In fact, they're really—well, really very beautiful.' And so they were, all those exquisitely carved bodies locked together in different forms of physical adoration. 'But why do they have those sorts of carvings here, in a temple?' she went on, curiosity taking the place of that brief flare of embarrassment.

'No one knows for certain,' Marcus told her, and Lacey's ears pricked up nervously as she heard a slightly husky undertone in his voice that she had never heard before. 'One theory is that they have their origins in the primitive religions of Nepal. Fertility was considered very important at that time, and the sexual act represented the continuation of life.'

Lacey stared at the erotically entwined figures with the first glimmerings of a new understanding. The continuation of life—yes, that made sense, she could see why the Nepalese had thought the act which sparked new life was so important that they had wanted to depict it on their temples.

A near by oil-lamp flickered, then burned a little brighter, and Marcus's shadow darkened, it was covering her own now, almost seeming to swallow it up. Lacey's attention drifted rapidly away from the carvings, there were other matters beginning to occupy her mind now, and the unease that had haunted her earlier started to return in full force.

She swallowed with some difficulty, her throat felt oddly tight. 'It's—it's getting late,' she somehow managed to get out. 'I suppose we should be getting back to the hotel.'

She glanced up nervously at Marcus, then found to her consternation that she couldn't look away again. As always, his slate-grey eyes were quite unreadable, but there was something about the fixed line of his mouth which warned her he was a very long way from being the cool, detached man she had worked for these past months.

It was almost like that moment when they had stood on the bank of the Ganges, surrounded by people but aware only of each other. Lacey couldn't help feeling a brief flash of resentment at what was happening, this acute physical response that had started to flare up between them, like a great blaze of light. It was as if someone was playing a lousy trick on them, and then standing back and laughing at their helplessness.

The lamp flickered again, briefly throwing the features of Marcus's face into sharp relief, and Lacey nervously licked her dry lips.

'Did you do that on purpose?' Marcus growled tersely.

'Do—do what?' she stuttered.

'Lick your lips like that?'

Lacey stared at him a little dazedly. It had been an involuntary gesture, that was all. So why did he sound so angry, why was he looking at her as if he were wishing it was *his* tongue that had run lightly and moistly over the soft outline of her mouth?

He kept staring at her so intensely that she felt his gaze would actually melt her if he kept it up much longer. Then he shifted his position slightly, and for an agonising couple of seconds she thought he was going to take another step forward, which would bring him within touching distance. Instead, though, he drew in a sudden sharp breath, then lifted his hands in a brief, frustrated gesture.

Without saying another word, he wheeled round and began to walk away. Lacey stared after him uneasily, then at last started to follow him, careful to keep a safe distance away from him so that there was no chance of their touching, even accidentally.

Completely oblivious to the crowds, to the forest of lamp-lit temples and the whirling dancers, they made

their way back through the streets and squares of
Kathmandu. When the hotel finally came into sight,
Lacey let out a silent sigh of relief. She was safe now; in
just a couple of minutes she could escape up to her room.
The dancing butterflies in her stomach gradually started
to settle down, and her racing pulses began to return to
something like normal.

They went up the stairs, and when they reached the
door to her room, Lacey paused a little uncertainly.
Should she say goodnight, or would it be better to go in
without saying a single word? And why was Marcus just
standing there, as if he couldn't quite decide what to do
next?

She glanced a little edgily along the corridor. It was
completely deserted, all the other doors were tightly
closed. And it was so silent, so still. They might almost
have been the only two people in the hotel. Or was it just
because she was with Marcus? Lacey wondered with a
fresh surge of apprehension. When he was standing this
close to her, everyone else seemed simply to fade into the
background, somehow to cease to exist.

Her gaze flickered up to him, then she couldn't look
away again because she had seen that expression on his
face before, at Varanasi, when he had slid a bright
orange marigold into her hair. There was no flower in her
hair now, but it didn't really make any difference; a
familiar weakness was spreading through all her limbs
and she was suddenly acutely aware of his surging
response.

Marcus lifted his hand, with just one finger he lightly
stroked a glistening strand of her dark red hair.

'Beautiful hair,' he murmured in a voice that was a
little hoarse, unexpectedly shaken. 'Do you know how
many times I've wanted to touch it? Run my hands

through its heavy warmth?'

Lacey couldn't move, with that one finger he held her fixed to the spot. All she could do was stare up at him with a mixture of nervousness and fascination. For several moments, he simply stared back, and his eyes definitely weren't unreadable now, they blazed brightly with a quite unmistakable message. *I want you. I don't like it, but that's the way it is, so what do we do about it?*

She had no idea how long they stood there, locked together by a force that neither of them even began to understand. Then Marcus's eyes suddenly flared even more brightly.

'Oh, what the hell!' he muttered thickly. He opened the door, seized her round the wrist, and pulled her roughly inside. Then he followed her in, and closed the door purposefully behind him.

CHAPTER FOUR

THE room was in near darkness, lit only by a pale beam of
moonlight filtering in through the unshuttered windows.
She could just see his dark male shape, the silvery gleam
of his hair, and the bright glitter of his eyes as he stared
down at her. His fingers were still locked firmly around
her wrists, he clearly had no intention of letting go of her,
and it never even occurred to her to try to struggle free. In
fact, her mind was frighteningly blank, only her body
seemed capable of any kind of definite response, and it
had begun to quiver tautly in a strange, unfamiliar
pattern of tiny inner tremors.

Marcus was leaning against the door, as if deliberately
blocking her only escape route. She felt his fingers press
hard against the soft inner skin of her wrist, and knew
that he could feel her racing pulse, she even heard his
quiet grunt of satisfaction as he registered the turbulent
response of her body to his touch.

'Why fight it?' he murmured a few moments later, and
she had the odd impression that he was talking to
himself, not to her. 'Why shouldn't I have what I want?'

Lacey shook her head numbly; this was wrong, she
didn't know why, but it was *wrong*, something inside her
head was screaming at her to be careful, not to let this go
too far. But Marcus's other hand had curled round her
wrist now, he was drawing her closer, and suddenly her
pulses were hammering away at a frightening speed. She
tried to say something, to force out a fierce protest, but
her voice just wouldn't work, nothing came out except a

choked little groan.

A wave of dizziness was sweeping over her, making her feel weak. She raised her head and gazed up at him in a mute appeal to let her go, to stop this insanity before it ran away with them, got totally out of hand and swallowed them up. Marcus didn't see her appeal, though—or perhaps he didn't want to see it, was deliberately closing his eyes to it. Instead, he bent his own head, and an instant later his mouth closed over hers.

The first touch of his lips seemed to send a jolt of pure sensation careering straight through her, she felt her body jerk as if it had received a fatal shock, even her heart seemed to stop beating for a few frantic seconds. Then it started up again with a crashing thud, its fast, heavy beat echoing in her ears, making her feel even more light-headed.

She swayed against him, not sure her legs would hold her up for much longer. And what she found was a hard male body already deep in the grip of intense desire.

His kiss deepened; there was nothing gentle about the assault of Marcus's lips, his tongue, as they broke through her feeble defences, then explored with arrogant assurance. The darkness somehow made his sensual exploration seem even more intimate; she couldn't see him properly, she could only feel what he was doing to her, feel her own extraordinary response as her body shook under his touch, wanting more and more of this delicious ravaging of every single one of her senses.

Marcus raised his head briefly, she heard him draw in a deep, shuddering breath, then another, as if he were finding it impossibly hard to hang on to the fragile threads of his self-control. Then he spun her round so that she was the one with her back to the door, and she could feel the hard wood pressing against her spine as he nipped her delicate skin lightly with his teeth, then caressed the tingling spot softly with his tongue, pain and pleasure mingling together with devastating effect.

'I didn't think anyone would ever get to me like this again,' he muttered roughly under his breath. 'I wouldn't *let* them get to me. But perhaps it won't matter, just this once——'

His words filtered through her dazed brain very slowly, it was several seconds before she even realised what he had said, before his last phrase finally registered in her conscious mind.

'Just this once——'

Without warning, there was a fierce explosion of memory inside her head, and all of a sudden she could hear the echo of a voice saying exactly the same thing. Only it wasn't Marcus who was speaking, the smooth coaxing tone belonged to a man she truly loathed and despised, a man who still sometimes haunted her dreams, turning them into nightmares.

'——come on, sweetheart, just this once. No one will ever know, your mother will never find out, I promise. Just this once——'

Lacey's head snapped up, for a few moments she couldn't even remember where she was, she was still drifting around in the past. Fingers were sliding up to caress the swollen, aching curve of her breast, but she didn't realise they belonged to Marcus, instead her mind was flooded with pictures of a tanned hand covered with a thin coating of coarse black hairs. Vittorio——

'No,' she muttered, a little wildly. The fingers didn't go away, though, they were actually rubbing against her even harder now, and she felt the first wave of panic rush over her. 'No!' she repeated with sudden vehemence.

Marcus instantly let go of her this time. A moment later, he snapped on the light; then he regarded her with eyes that had gone hard and cold.

'If you meant all along to say no, then you should have said it loudly and clearly at the very beginning,' he told her, his tense voice warning her that the controlled façade was just a front, inside he was still tightly wound up, hovering on the very edge of an explosion of temper and frustration.

Confused, Lacey shook her head. 'I didn't mean——' she began unsteadily, but then she stopped, she wasn't at all sure *what* she had meant. The last few minutes had become hopelessly mixed up inside her head, past and present had somehow blurred together, right now she couldn't sort one out from the other.

A dark stain of colour still edged Marcus's cheekbones, and he was starting to look as if he would dearly like to wring her neck. He swung away from her, prowled restlessly over to the far side of the room, then turned back to face her.

'I suppose I ought to thank you,' he growled tersely at last. 'You've just saved us from making a very bad mistake.' Lacey tried to say something, but he swiftly held up his hand, the curt gesture instantly warning her to stay silent. 'We'll discuss this in the morning,' he went on, his tone still totally grim. 'Perhaps by then we'll both be feeling a little more—rational. Goodnight, Lacey.'

He strode over to the door, then left without saying another word. Lacey didn't know if she was glad to see him go or not. She walked shakily over to the bed, then collapsed down on to it. A moment later, she gave a violent shiver. If Marcus hadn't unwittingly said those three small words, there was every likelihood he would be on this bed with her right now. She might not have had a

lot of practical experience where men were concerned,
but she could certainly recognise raw desire when she
saw it. And for a while, to her amazement, she had been
equally carried away. She had never thought it could
happen to her like that, she had always been on her guard
against it, utterly determined to avoid the sexual tricks
her body could play on her.

That was why she had decided long ago that she didn't
ever want to get involved with a man like Marcus
Caradin. She had met his type so many times before, they
had marched in and out of her mother's life with
monotonous regularity. Her mother might have found all
that charm and high-powered sex appeal quite irresistible, but Lacey had deliberately closed her mind to it, she
had remained singularly unimpressed. She hadn't wanted to get caught up in all the dramatic highs and lows that
had ruled her mother's existence; living with her mother
had provided enough second-hand excitement to last
anyone a lifetime. And for the last couple of years she
had got exactly what she had wanted: a quiet, steady life-
style that had suited her down to the ground, and which
she had expected to go on indefinitely. Only now Marcus
Caradin was threatening to rip it all to pieces with the
touch of his mouth and his clever, clever hands.

Lacey gave a small groan and closed her eyes. Then she
immediately opened them again because pictures of
Vittorio kept flickering behind her shut eyelids, she
couldn't seem to stop herself drifting even further back
into the past. Her face darkened into a scowl. That rat! If
it hadn't been for him, she and her mother wouldn't have
gone through that emotional break-up, they would all
have been saved a lot of hassle and heartache.

Then she let out a deep sigh. She supposed if she was
going to be strictly honest with herself, Vittorio hadn't

been entirely to blame for what had happened. It had been building up for quite a long time before that, but Lacey had deliberately turned a blind eye to it, she hadn't wanted to admit that the relationship between her and her mother was becoming distinctly strained.

Not that it had been like that for most of her life, of course. Marie Harrison had been very fond of her daughter in a rather haphazard sort of way, and she had given Lacey as much affection as she had to spare. Lacey was well aware that a lot of people considered her mother's morals left a lot to be desired, but her nature, although rather shallow, had been basically generous—too generous, Lacey had thought to herself ruefully on more than one occasion. It was a good job Lacey had turned out to be practical by nature. As she had grown older, she had gradually taken charge of her mother's erratic, chaotic life-style and brought some kind of order into it. She even dealt with their finances, eking out their small private income that came from some shares her father had left them, juggling the bills as they came in, paying the more urgent ones on a strict rotation basis and becoming very adept at keeping all their other creditors at bay. It was probably what made her such an efficient secretary, she had told herself later, more than once. Running a small office was nothing after years of coping with her mother's frantically muddled life-style.

And it *had* been muddled. Two marriages, two divorces, and Lacey had long ago lost track of all the brief but intense affairs there had been in between. Her mother seemed to fall in and out of love almost as often as ordinary people ate hot dinners. And there had never been a chance to settle anywhere, they were always on the move, sometimes staying with one of her mother's endless list of friends, occasionally renting a room, but more often than not moving in with some smoothly sophisticated man for a few months—or even just a few weeks, if things didn't turn out too well. So many charming, handsome men had drifted in and out of her life that Lacey often found it hard to remember the names that went with them.

During those restless, unsettled years, adolescence came and went for Lacey, but it didn't seem to bring any miraculous changes. The thin child turned into a thin teenager, and her carrot-red hair blazed as brightly as ever, attracting all the usual nicknames. It wasn't until she was nearly twenty that she looked in the mirror one day and realised, with a dawning sense of shock, that something a bit odd seemed to be happening to her. Her hair was darkening to a rich, rather exotic shade of red, and by contrast her eyes somehow seemed even greener, shining with an almost feline quality beneath the long, thick lashes. Even her bone structure looked different, more delicately defined, slightly fragile.

But it was her body that seemed to be altering the most. Her breasts, fairly small until now, were filling out, she actually had to go out and buy some new bras because the old ones were too small. And there was a new sleekness to her hips and legs, she could feel the change when she walked, her body had started to move in an entirely new way, as if it wanted to show itself off to its best advantage.

'You must be a late developer,' she muttered to herself one day as she stepped out of the bath and ran her fingers lightly over her wet, supple skin, feeling the full and unfamiliar curves. Yet there had been a faint note of unease in her voice because, although she didn't want to admit it to herself, she knew that her mother, too, had begun to notice the changes in her. Noticed them, and not particularly liked them.

The trouble began in a small way at first. When the two of them walked into a restaurant, occasionally the unthinkable would happen and men's eyes would swivel round to fix on Lacey instead of going directly to her mother, as had always happened in the past. And then there was the attitude of her mother's boyfriends. Instead of ignoring her, or at best treating her with casual politeness, they began to look at her in an entirely different way, their experienced, calculating gazes resting on her in a way that was quite unmistakable.

'Really, darling, having a grown-up daughter like you around all the time is beginning to make me feel quite middle-aged,' her mother remarked one day in a distinctly brittle tone. Deeply disturbed, Lacey muttered some excuse and left the room. It was the first time her mother had ever said such a thing, she usually insisted that she simply couldn't manage without Lacey to organise her life for her. Her mother's dependence on her was the main reason why Lacey had put up so long with a way of life that was very different from the one she really wanted for herself.

Then they moved to Florence, and that was when Vittorio came into their lives. Vittorio—prize charmer, prize macho man—prize rat! And to Lacey's astonishment, her mother had really gone overboard for him, she positively sparkled every time he walked into the room, went into a deep depression if he had to go away on business for a couple of days, moped for hours if he didn't ring when he had promised.

To Lacey, it was a complete mystery why her mother considered Vittorio so special. He really didn't seem any different from all the other men who had drifted in and out of Marie's life. Dark-haired and dark-eyed, he had

the same air of wealth and sophistication that her mother
always went for, that seemed to draw her like a magnet,
Privately, Lacey was certain Vittorio was a phoney, that
the charm was false and his bank balance was as
precarious as their own. She knew better than to criticise
him, though, while Marie was still flying high on this
latest grand passion. All she could do was sit it out, wait
for the affair to run its course, like all the others. Then
Vittorio would finally clear off out of their lives, and she
could forget about him.

   Lacey shivered. It hadn't worked out like that, Vittorio
had had a far greater impact on her life than she could
ever have anticipated. And with that one short little
phrase—'Just this once'—Marcus had brought it all
flooding back into her mind again, for a while there she
had even got the two of them mixed up inside her head.
She was well aware that she was being completely unfair
to Marcus. Whatever else he might be, he certainly
couldn't be put in the same category as Vittorio, but she
was finding it almost impossible to think straight
tonight. Vittorio—Marcus—she shook her head confu-
sedly, her mind felt as if it were spinning giddily round
and round in circles.

   A loud knock on the door suddenly broke through into
her turbulent thoughts. She sat bolt upright, then
nervously chewed her bottom lip. She didn't want to see
or talk to anyone again tonight, and certainly not to
Marcus. And she was sure it was him on the other side of
the door. Who else could it be? Perhaps if she kept very
quiet, he would think she had fallen asleep, and would go
away again.

   Then she let out a small sigh. Marcus Caradin wasn't a
man who would ever walk way from anything. And as if
to prove her right, he didn't even bother to knock a

second time, he simply opened her door, then strode into the centre of the room. For a moment, he just stood there looking at her intently, and Lacey nervously noted the bright glitter of his eyes.

'I've decided that this can't wait until morning,' he informed her at last, very crisply. 'We've got to discuss this right now, then make some definite decisions about the future.'

Lacey knew she ought to order him out of her room, or at least make a vehement protest at this invasion of her privacy. The sight of him standing there, gold hair gleaming, his features set in a hard frown, his body noticeably tense, was enough to strike her totally dumb, and she wondered a little hysterically how on earth they were going to talk this over when her throat was quite frozen.

'I've no intention of apologising for what happened earlier,' he went on, his voice even curter now. 'In fact, if anyone's going to offer an apology, I think it ought to be you. Or if not an apology, at least an explanation.'

That definitely freed her paralysed throat. 'An apology?' she repeated, with a sudden surge of indignation. 'An *explanation*? Do I really have to give you a reason why I wouldn't jump into bed with you? Perhaps you'd like it in writing,' she went on with growing sarcasm. 'Then you could file it for future reference!'

As she saw the dark expression that instantly spread over his face, it occurred to her that perhaps she had gone a little too far. Well, too bad! she decided furiously. It was the middle of the night, she was tired and upset, and she definitely didn't need this sort of hassle right now.

Then, to her surprise, his face cleared again, and he visibly relaxed. Moving over to the far side of the room, he settled himself into a chair, then he sat back and looked at her.

'One way or the other, the last few days have been full of surprises,' he remarked, raising one gold eyebrow thoughtfully. 'For the past year, I've considered you to be the perfect secretary. Always efficient, always calm, always in control—it was virtually impossible to find fault with you.'

'Isn't that what you wanted?' she retaliated instantly. 'Someone who would run the office smoothly, and cope with all the minor crises?'

'That's precisely what I wanted,' Marcus agreed. 'And you fitted the bill perfectly. But these last few days have been something of a revelation. Apparently you can also be irritable, sarcastic, and downright bad-tempered.'

'Everyone's got a few faults,' she muttered.

The corners of his mouth lifted into a dry smile. 'Believe it or not, it's rather a relief to discover you're actually human. Sometimes I used to get the impression you were just too perfect to be real.' But then his smile faded away again, and the beginnings of a light frown took its place. 'But it's got its disadvantages, too,' he went on in a more sombre tone. 'Seeing you in a new light hasn't really worked out well for either of us, it's triggered off a lot of problems that it's getting harder and harder to deal with. I don't think we can go on like this, Lacey. One way or another, we've got to get our working relationship straightened out.'

She stared at him slightly belligerently. 'You're making it sound as if everything that's happened has been my fault,' she accused. 'And I don't think that's the case. Anyway,' she went on, 'you're the boss, you're meant to be in charge—what do *you* think we ought to do about it?'

'I can think of at least one very simple solution to the situation,' he replied. 'But before I discuss it with you, I want to get back to what we were talking about earlier. I meant it when I told you I wanted an explanation for the way you behaved. I didn't hurt you, I didn't force you, and you certainly didn't seem unwilling to go along with what was happening. So why did you suddenly freeze up on me like that? Have you got some sexual hang-up? Are you scared of men—or of me?'

'Definitely not!' Lacey denied instantly, and was furious to find herself going bright scarlet. 'I just didn't— didn't want to get involved with you.'

Marcus nodded. 'I can appreciate that. Despite what happened tonight, I feel precisely the same way. But why the hell didn't you say so earlier? Why did you let it go that far?'

'Why did you?' she retorted.

He began to look rather tense again. 'Things got— slightly out of hand. I never intended anything like that to happen. In certain situations, though, we just seem to strike sparks off each other. It's just as well you stopped me when you did, or we'd probably have been in a real mess by now. But I get the feeling you still haven't told me the whole truth about *why* you stopped me.'

Lacey sighed. He wasn't going to give up on this until he had squeezed a full explanation out of her. Perhaps it would be better just to tell him, and get it over with. She didn't think she could face much more of this verbal sparring, not tonight.

'It was something you said,' she admitted reluctantly. 'You probably don't even remember it. You said, "Just this once——".'

Marcus frowned. 'And you thought I was after a one-night stand? A couple of hours in bed, and then we'd both forget all about it?'

'No, it wasn't that,' Lacey cut in quickly. 'What you said—well, it reminded me of someone else who'd said exactly the same thing.' Marcus's eyes swiftly darkened, but this time he remained silent. 'His name was Vittorio,' Lacey went on, after a brief pause. 'He was one of my mother's boyfriends. Dark and smooth and good-looking——' She shuddered expressively. 'I couldn't stand him!'

She saw surprise instantly register on Marcus's face. 'But I thought——' Then he stopped. 'No, it doesn't matter. Go on.'

Lacey looked at him with sudden understanding. 'You thought I was in love with him?'

He shrugged. 'It seemed a fairly obvious conclusion.'

'Well, I definitely wasn't!' she assured him vehemently. 'It's my mother who goes for the Latin types, not me. In fact, she's living with an Italian dress-designer right now, she's been with him for nearly a year—which is practically a record,' she added drily. 'Although come to think of it, there are one or two advantages. She keeps sending me outfits from his latest collection, and he really is a fantastic designer.'

'Lacey, you're wandering away from the subject,' Marcus reminded her. Then he glanced at her sharply. 'Are you doing it on purpose? Do you really not want to talk about it?'

She sighed. 'I might as well tell you, it's not *that* terrible. Looking back, I suppose it was even rather predictable. I must have been pretty thick not to have seen it coming.'

'Or pretty innocent,' Marcus commented, in an unexpectedly harsh voice.

Lacey grimaced. 'I was certainly hopelessly naïve

where Vittorio was concerned. I mean, I knew he used to watch me sometimes when he thought I wasn't looking, but I never thought——' She stopped, and her eyes shadowed over. 'You can probably guess what happened,' she went on a few moments later, in a low voice. 'My mother was out with some friends one evening, and Vittorio came back earlier than expected from a business trip. As soon as he found out we were going to be on our own for a few hours, he jumped on me.' She shuddered violently at the memory. 'He was disgusting, he seemed to be all hands and mouth. The more I struggled, the more it seemed to turn him on, and all the time he kept saying that it would be all right, he'd make sure my mother never found out if I'd let him do it just this once— as if that was all that really mattered, not being found out!'

Marcus's eyes narrowed tensely. 'What happened? Did he——?'

'No, thank God,' Lacey answered with some fervour. 'Though what happened was nearly as bad. I got to the point where I just couldn't fight him any more, he was incredibly strong and I felt so suffocated, I thought I was going to pass right out. Everything started to go black, I more or less collapsed in his arms, he practically had to hold me up. It didn't stop him, of course, in another few moments he'd have shoved me down on to the sofa and that would have been that, but for just those few seconds I was draped all over him and I wasn't fighting him. You get the picture?' As Marcus nodded grimly, Lacey went on, 'And at that precise moment, my mother returned early and walked in on the two of us.'

Marcus frowned. 'But surely she didn't believe——?'

'Vittorio made sure he got in first with his version of what had happened,' Lacey replied, rather wearily. 'He

said he'd had too much to drink, that I'd led him on and
he'd lost control, and he was sorry, so sorry, he wanted to
die of shame——' She paused. 'It was all very dramatic,'
she recalled contemptuously. 'At one point he even flung
himself on his knees and begged forgiveness. It was quite
a scene—someone should have awarded him an Oscar
for it.'

'And your mother swallowed the entire story?'

Lacey gave a resigned shrug of her shoulders. 'She
wanted to believe it. She was totally infatuated with
Vittorio, she'd have believed just about anything as long
as it meant she could hold on to him.'

Marcus's features were still set in a hard, dark frown.
'Someone ought to have shaken your mother until her
brain started functioning normally again! What the hell
kind of person could take a stranger's word against her
own daughter's?'

'It wasn't really my mother's fault,' Lacey jumped in
defensively. 'She can't help being the way she is, it's
just—well, a sort of flaw in her character. If you knew
her, you'd understand that. You just have to love her and
accept her the way she is. Anyway, in a funny way it all
worked out for the best in the long run. We were already
getting near the point where it was time for me to leave
home. This simply hurried things along a bit. I moved to
London, took a secretarial course, and after a couple of
temporary jobs ended up at Caradin Tours.'

'What happened to Vittorio?'

She gave a rueful grin. 'A few months later, my mother
dumped him. Apparently his charm wore thin fairly fast.
She went off with an oilman from Texas after that, then
moved on to the Italian dress-designer who's so kindly
building up my wardrobe. And once Vittorio was out of
the way, my mother and I eventually managed to patch

things up between us. It's not quite the same as it was before, of course, but at least we're not getting along too badly on the rare occasions that we meet.'

Marcus shook his head bemusedly. 'I'd no idea you had such a colourful background. On the other hand, I knew that something out of the ordinary had happened tonight. I might not be the world's greatest lover, but women don't usually freeze up completely in my arms.'

No, I bet they don't! Lacey thought with some feeling. And who was Marcus trying to kid, running himself down like that? If they were running a competition for Lover of the Year, she was absolutely certain Marcus Caradin would end up near the very top of the list.

'On the other hand,' he went on, his voice suddenly growing appreciably cooler, 'if you've somehow linked me with Vittorio in your mind, that could very well solve a lot of our problems. No one in their right mind would want to get involved with someone who reminded them of a traumatic episode in their past.' He paused briefly, then stared at her with dark intensity. 'Do you really think of us as being similar, Lacey?'

She could tell from his harsh tone of voice that he hadn't wanted to ask that last question, and her first impulse was to jump in and deny it emphatically.

Then she found herself hesitating. Of course, they were totally different in so many ways, not least in appearance. Vittorio had been so dark while Marcus was all bright, glittering hair and cool grey eyes. And there was no chance that Marcus would ever behave in the same way as Vittorio, she would stake just about everything on that. And yet—there *was* the very faintest of similarities, that invisible aura of power, of self-confidence, of a rather awesome level of sexual expertise. The only thing was, in Vittorio it had been completely phoney, while in Marcus she was absolutely certain it was a hundred per cent genuine.

'Well——' she began awkwardly at last, but he didn't give her a chance to get any further.

'All right, I'll spare you the embarrassment of having to say it out loud,' he told her tersely. 'I'm quite capable of drawing my own conclusions.'

She was about to rush in and tell him that he was wrong, that she had only hesitated because she was still trying to sort it all out in her own mind, when she suddenly stopped. Perhaps it would be better to leave things exactly as they were. If she didn't want to get involved with Marcus—and despite everything that had happened, she was still certain that she didn't—then it definitely wouldn't hurt to leave him with the wrong impression. It was hardly fair, of course, but at least it would provide a solution to what was getting to be a very awkward situation.

But that still left one basic question to be answered. Could they still work together? It didn't take her long to reach the firm conclusion that they could. They would both have to make a major effort, but she was convinced they could work things out, if they really wanted to. After all, hadn't he told her more than once that she was a sensible girl? All she had to do was to apply some of that common sense, and everything could go back to being exactly the way it had been before.

Marcus's thoughts were obviously moving very much in the same direction, but it soon became clear that he had reached a very different conclusion.

'If I remind you of Vittorio, then in theory that should rule out any kind of relationship between us, as far as you're concerned,' he said curtly. 'And I've got my own reasons for not wanting to get involved. I've no intention of going into them right now, they're personal, but believe me, the very last thing I want is to get caught up in an affair with you.'

'Then it doesn't look as if we're going to have too many problems,' Lacey responded rather stiffly.

Marcus leant forward slightly. 'But what we both want doesn't seem to cut much ice when we're thrown together in a certain type of situation,' he reminded her, with some acerbity. 'For some reason, we've developed a very strong physical response towards one another. And we don't seem to have very much control over it. It's extremely inconvenient that it should have happened right now——'

'Inconvenient!' she cut in, slightly incredulously.

His grey eyes regarded her coolly. 'How else would you describe it?'

With an effort, she got control of herself again. 'All right,' she answered, somehow forcing her voice to stay calm and steady, 'what do you suggest we should do about it?'

'The obvious solution is for you to go directly back to England,' he answered evenly.

Instantly incensed, she jumped to her feet. 'Why should *I* be the one to return home?' she demanded. 'That's tantamount to saying the whole thing's my fault, so I'm the one who's got to be packed off back to the office.'

Marcus's hands moved in a sudden gesture of impatience. 'I'm simply looking at the situation from a purely practical point of view,' he replied, a rather terse note creeping into his voice. 'There's still a lot of work to be done before this holiday tour's set up. All the arrangements have got to be made for the last half of this trip to Nepal, and you don't have the experience yet to cope with it. It makes sense that I should be the one to stay here and finish the job.'

Lacey was willing to concede that made sense, but she was on her guard now, she was beginning to realise there were a lot more questions that still had to be answered.

'And what will happen when I get back to England?' she asked suspiciously.

'What do you mean?'

Was he being deliberately naïve because he didn't want to talk about it? Well, she wasn't going to let him get away with that!

'I mean, how is working in the office going to be any different from working together on this field trip?' she demanded bluntly. 'What guarantee is there that we're not going to run into precisely the same kind of problems?'

Marcus lifted his head and regarded her levelly. 'Absolutely none,' he answered concisely. 'That's why it might be more beneficial if you considered looking for another job. I'd give you excellent references, of course, you shouldn't have any problem finding something suitable.'

Lacey could hardly believe what she was hearing. She glared back at him, her green eyes blazing with indignation. 'So you think it would be more beneficial, do you? But more beneficial for whom? For you, presumably,' she went on angrily, answering her own question, 'since it certainly isn't going to benefit me to give up a well paid job that I like.'

His own eyes began to glitter warningly. 'I'm merely trying to be practical,' he reminded her tersely.

'Oh yes, of course,' she agreed, her voice now dripping with sarcasm. 'You want *me* to go back to England, you want *me* to give up my job. I'm sure that's a very practical solution as far as you're concerned. After all,' she flung at him furiously, 'it means that *you* don't have to give up anything at all.'

He got to his feet and strode towards her, and for one fraught moment she thought he was actually going to shake her. Then he swung away from her again, muttering darkly under his breath, and like a blinding flash it dawned on her that he was afraid to touch her, that even now, in the middle of this blazing row, he didn't fully trust himself, he wouldn't risk any physical contact between them. That thought sharply sobered her for a few moments; but then she was instantly on her guard again as he turned back to confront her, letting her see the rigid determination on his face.

'I don't see any other solution to the problem,' he told her rather grimly. 'What else do you expect me to do? Give up my own job? I'd remind you, Lacey, that I own Caradin Tours. And that gives me a certain advantage in this situation, wouldn't you say?'

Her head came up, and her eyes blazed scornfully into his own. 'I'd say that gave you every advantage,' she agreed, making absolutely no effort to keep a note of deep contempt out of her voice. 'And you're obviously going to use it to push me out of a perfectly good job.'

For a moment, she thought she had provoked him too far. Amazed at her own courage, at the way she had stood up to this man she had always regarded with just a touch of awe, she took a step back and felt her limbs begin to quiver slightly with nervous reaction.

Marcus swung away from her and stared out of the window for several long, tense seconds. From the rigid set of his shoulder-blades, it was obvious that he was making a huge effort to bring his own temper back under control. When he eventually turned back to face her, though, it was clear he had succeeded because his grey eyes had taken on the cool expression with which she was so familiar, and his taut features had been wiped clean of all trace of emotion.

He could be so frighteningly controlled, so cold-blooded, Lacey thought to herself with a small shiver. She supposed it was what made him so successful in business. Soulless, she had called him once, and she was beginning to think she had been right, that was precisely what he was.

'My mind's made up on this point,' he told her shortly. 'I'll arrange your flight back home first thing in the morning. Once this trip is over and I've returned to England myself, we'll try to reach some mutually satisfactory agreement about your future career.'

'In other words, you're going to sack me,' she retorted bluntly. 'Well, let's get one thing straight right now. I've no intention of losing my job because of something that isn't my fault. Just try it, and I'll go directly to the industrial tribunal and claim that I was unfairly dismissed!'

Marcus stared at her in blank disbelief. 'Are you blackmailing me?' he demanded incredulously, as if he couldn't believe anyone would have the nerve to do such a thing.

Lacey almost laughed out loud with sheer nervousness. It must have been years since anyone had dared to stand up to Marcus Caradin like this, and it was pretty obvious he wasn't liking it one little bit. Why should she be the one to suffer, though, because of this physical attraction that had so unexpectedly, so inconveniently sprung up between them? In this sort of situation, it was always the woman, the lowly secretary, who was expected to compromise, to give way, she thought resentfully. The fact that she had been thinking about changing her job anyway had suddenly become quite irrelevant. It was a matter of principle now, she was grimly determined to hang on to her job, no matter what it took.

Marcus had already turned his back on her, though, and was striding towards the door.

'This is getting us absolutely nowhere,' he muttered angrily. 'We'll discuss it again in the morning. Perhaps you'll be in a more reasonable mood by then.'

'I shan't have changed my mind!' she flung at him warningly, but it was too late, he had already left and hadn't heard her.

Lacey prowled restlessly round the room for a couple of minutes, too strung up to keep still, then finally slumped on the edge of the bed and stared broodingly at the opposite wall.

What a crazy, mixed-up evening it had been. Her head was positively reeling, and it didn't look as if tomorrow was going to be any easier to cope with.

She gave a ragged sigh, wished she could conjure up a sleeping pill that would knock her out for a few hours, then resignedly prepared herself for a sleepless night.

CHAPTER FIVE

By morning, she had calmed down considerably and could look at the whole situation much more calmly and unemotionally. In fact, she was ready to admit that she had over-reacted to some degree, a lot of the things Marcus had said had made quite a lot of sense.

Not that she was ready to go along with *everything* he had suggested, Lacey reminded herself with some determination. She definitely didn't intend to pack in her job and just meekly walk away from Caradin Tours. But she could see that this particular trip wasn't working out, for some reason they didn't seem able to keep up the proper boss/secretary relationship once they were away from the office. And Marcus had been right on another point, she didn't have enough experience to cope on her own with all the work involved in setting up a new holiday tour. It made sense that he should be the one to stay on and finish this job.

She had finally decided that what was needed was a compromise solution, and she had worked one out during her sleepless night. All she had to do now was to put it to him. She was ready to agree to fly back to England as soon as he could arrange a ticket for her, but she definitely wasn't going to resign. Once they were back in the office, in a formal working environment, she was certain everything would soon get back to normal, there wouldn't be any more of those—well, those flare-ups that had started to erupt between them, she told herself, feeling a touch of heat creeping into her skin as uncomfortably vivid memories suddenly flashed into her mind. There would be no more marigolds, no magic sunrises and *definitely* no hard, urgent kisses.

With that decided, she quickly showered and dressed, then went along to tap lightly on Marcus's door. It was still early, but she wanted to tell him about her decision as soon as possible. That would give him plenty of time to make all the arrangements for her return home.

There wasn't any answer, so she knocked again, then wondered if he had already gone downstairs. It was far too early for breakfast, the dining-room wouldn't be open for at least another half-hour, but perhaps, like her, he hadn't been able to sleep and had gone for a walk——

A little nervously, she silently turned the handle, then pushed the door open just a couple of inches. If he was still in bed, then she certainly didn't want to wake him and have him see her peering into his bedroom. She could just imagine what his reaction would be!

She let out a brief sigh of relief when she saw the bed was empty. She was just about to close the door again when she noticed a couple of the drawers in the unit beside the bed were half open, and their contents were piled up higgledy-piggledy. Lacey frowned, she knew Marcus was meticulously tidy and methodical in the office, it didn't make sense for his room to be in such a mess.

Then she saw the pair of feet sticking out from behind the bed.

Swallowing hard, Lacey tip-toed further into the room, then forced herself to peer apprehensively over the edge of the mattress. A second later, she let out a strangled squeak of alarm. The feet belonged to Marcus, he was sprawled out on the floor on the other side of the bed, and there was a messy trickle of blood staining his bright gold hair.

For a few seconds, she completely panicked. Flinging herself down beside him, she gave a low moan of anguish as she searched frantically for signs of life but couldn't find any. Then her fluttering fingers located a pulse beating slowly but strongly in his throat. Lacey briefly flopped back with sheer relief. At least he was alive. He was out cold, though, and showing absolutely no signs of coming round.

Scrambling to her feet, she lunged for the phone. After getting through to the switchboard, she made it clear there would be dire consequences if they didn't get a doctor here in five minutes flat. Then she went back to crouch anxiously beside Marcus, wishing she knew something about first aid so that she could do something useful instead of just staring at him helplessly, her fingers twisting together with anxiety.

'Marcus? Marcus! Damn it, why won't you open your eyes?' she muttered frustratedly as the minutes ticked by and he continued to lie frighteningly still.

It seemed to take hours for the doctor to arrive, although in reality it was probably no more than ten minutes. He finally strode into the room, a tall, rather lanky man, closely followed by a short, dark, worried-looking man whom Lacey recognised as the manager of the hotel.

The doctor immediately knelt beside Marcus. 'What did he do, fall out of bed?' he commented, lightly raising one eyebrow. Then he peered a little closer. 'No, I can see it's rather more serious than that.'

Lacey hovered anxiously just inches away. 'Is he going to be all right?'

The doctor shot her a dry look. 'Since I don't have a crystal ball with me, that's a little hard to say at the moment. Anyway, I'm only qualified to give a diagnosis, not a reading of the future. And you'll only get that diagnosis if you'll stand back and let me have a look at him.'

'Sorry,' muttered Lacey. 'It's just that I'm so worried——'

'There's probably no need to be,' the doctor assured her, running his hands expertly over Marcus. 'This one looks pretty tough, I should think it would take more than a knock on the head to do any real damage. Hmm,' he went on, a few minutes later, 'I can't find anything that's bruised or broken, so let's get him on the bed and make him more comfortable, then I'll take a look at that cut on his head.' He turned to the hotel manager. 'Give me a hand, will you?'

The two of them lifted Marcus on to the bed, then the doctor's fingers threaded expertly through Marcus's gold hair. Lacey shuddered as his hands became streaked with blood, and he glanced up at her, giving an encouraging smile.

'Don't worry too much about the blood, head wounds always bleed like the devil and look far worse than they actually are. If there's going to be any real trouble, it'll be further down, in his actual skull. There's no obvious sign of any fracture, but we need to get him to hospital for a complete medical check-up.'

'No!'

The one word was faint, but very clear and very firm. And the voice definitely belonged to Marcus.

He hadn't opened his eyes yet, but he had gingerly begun to stir now, as if checking he was still in one piece.

'Don't move too much,' instructed the doctor. 'Can you open your eyes?' Marcus obliged, his grey gaze a little fuzzy at first, but rapidly clearing as he focused on the world around him. 'All right,' continued the doctor, 'how many fingers am I holding up?'

'Three,' answered Marcus without hesitation.

'What day is it?'

'Wednesday.'

'And do you remember your name?'

Lacey saw small lines of irritation begin to show at the corners of Marcus's mouth, and she gave a sigh of relief. He probably had a thundering headache, but he was obviously beginning to feel better.

'What the hell's going on here?' he demanded, his voice getting stronger by the second. 'Lacey, what's happened?'

'We've been waiting for you to tell *us* that,' she answered. 'I came in and found you flat out on the floor, with blood pouring out of your head. I thought you were dead!'

'Well, quite obviously I'm not,' Marcus responded drily. 'I've got a bloody awful headache, that's all.'

'It could be more serious than that,' the doctor cautioned. 'The cut itself's quite small, it probably won't even need stitches, but there's quite a sizable bump underneath. I'll phone the hospital straight away, then we can get you over there and have it checked out.'

'No,' Marcus said absolutely decisively, for the second time. 'Once a hospital gets its hands on you, they won't let you out until they've put you through every test they can think of. I don't have the time to spare for all that.'

The doctor began to look rather severe. 'A blow on the head should always be taken seriously,' he warned. 'You could have a hairline fracture that would only show up on an X-ray. And of course, there's always the possibility of concussion.'

Marcus growled irritably. 'All right,' he conceded with obvious reluctance. 'You can fix up a couple of X-rays for me. But it'll have to be as an out-patient, I'm not going to be admitted.'

'It's your head, not mine,' the doctor grunted. 'But provided the X-rays are clear, you shouldn't have too many problems as long as you're careful. You'll have to stay in bed for the rest of the week, of course. And if you get any nausea, any dizziness, any persistent headaches, then call me at once.'

'I'll stay in bed today,' Marcus agreed, with a definite lack of enthusiasm. 'And I'll try and take it easy tomorrow. But the day after that, I'm leaving for Pokhara.'

'Oh, no,' vetoed the doctor immediately, 'I couldn't possibly allow you to go on a long, tiring bus ride like that.'

'He isn't going to take the bus,' Lacey said wryly. 'He's going to walk.'

The doctor's thin eyebrows shot up. 'Impossible!'

'Just watch me,' answered Marcus calmly.

The doctor turned to Lacey. 'Your husband is a very stubborn man.'

'He isn't my husband,' she replied, flushing slightly. 'But he certainly is very stubborn,' she added.

The doctor shrugged. 'Well, short of chaining you to the bed, I can't stop you going. Personally, I think you're crazy, but that's only a professional medical opinion, of course. I'll write you a prescription that'll help to ease the pain in your head, and I'll arrange for you to have the X-rays this afternoon.'

'You still haven't told us how you *got* the knock on the head,' Lacey reminded Marcus. 'Did someone hit you?'

'I think they must have done,' Marcus nodded, with a grimace. 'I don't really remember very much. I went out early for a walk, came back into the room, and then went out like a light. I've got a vague memory of hearing footsteps behind me just before it happened, so I suppose I must have disturbed someone going through my room.'

The hotel manager stepped forward, looking distinctly unhappy. 'We've had several thefts from hotel rooms during the past couple of weeks,' he admitted. 'From the look of your room, I think you must have walked in on the thief while he was stealing your belongings. Do you know if anything's missing?'

'I haven't had much chance to check yet,' Marcus reminded him with some acerbity. 'And right now, I don't feel much like jumping up off this bed to take an inventory.'

Lacey heard the clear note of frustration in his voice, and understood it perfectly. He felt at a distinct disadvantage, lying there with his head aching and whirling, and it was already making him highly irritable. He wasn't used to being helpless, and he didn't like it in the least.

'Perhaps we ought to clear out and leave you alone for a while,' she suggested quickly. 'You probably want to get some rest.'

'I'll leave you a couple of pills you can take right away,' the doctor told him, 'and you can collect the rest of the prescription when you go to the hospital for the X-rays. And you'd better keep a close eye on him,' he added, turning to Lacey, 'just in case he develops any of the symptoms of concussion.'

'I don't need a nurse!' Marcus growled instantly.

The doctor looked as if he would dearly like to tell him exactly what he did need, but with an obvious effort he restrained himself, then allowed Lacey to usher him and the manager out of the room.

'I meant it about keeping an eye on him,' the doctor repeated firmly again, as soon as they were outside the door. 'And not just today. It's quite possible to get delayed concussion some time after the actual blow on the head. He shouldn't even get out of bed for the next few days, let alone go tramping off through the foothills of the Himalayas. If he really is insane enough to insist on going, then it's absolutely essential that someone should go with him.'

Lacey groaned inwardly because she knew at once who that 'someone' would have to be. So much for her plans for flying back to England. It looked as if Marcus was about to get a nurse he didn't want, and she was going to be stuck in Nepal for a few more days yet. She wasn't thrilled by the prospect, and she guessed Marcus was going to be even less enthusiastic about the whole idea. Altogether, the future suddenly seemed to be depressingly bleak.

'You are *not* coming to Pokhara.'

Lacey sighed. She had had a very busy couple of days, she was tired, and she could well do without all this aggravation.

'I really don't see how you can stop me,' she pointed out.

Marcus was sitting in the chair, looking pale and tired, but totally determined. The results of the X-rays had come through a couple of hours ago, there was no trace of any hairline fracture, so he was going ahead with his plans for the trek to Pokhara. And reluctantly following the doctor's instructions, Lacey was resigned to going with him every step of the way.

'I employ you,' Marcus reminded her. 'In my book, that gives me the right to tell you what you can or can't do during working hours.'

'Yes, you employ me,' she agreed. 'But that doesn't mean I have to obey your instructions like a robot!'

'Then I'll simply fire you,' he threatened flatly.

Lacey shrugged. 'Please yourself. It won't make the slightest difference. I'll still be tagging along behind you when you set off for Pokhara.'

Marcus ran his fingers through his hair in frustrated disbelief. 'My God, what do I have to do to get rid of you?'

'Give up the insane idea of going on this trek,' she answered instantly.

'I came out here to do a job, and I'm going to finish it,' he said with stubborn determination. 'But I can do it by myself, I don't need you to hold my hand.'

'No,' she agreed, 'but you might need someone to fetch help if you suddenly get hit by delayed concussion.'

'That won't happen!'

'It probably won't. I certainly *hope* it won't. But if it does, at least you'll have someone with you,' Lacey told him very firmly.

Seeing that Marcus seemed to have temporarily run out of arguments, she slumped back wearily in her chair. For the last couple of days, she had been doing all the things that Marcus had planned to do himself: inspecting local hotels, investigating local transport facilities, trudging round tourist highspots and generally preparing all the groundwork for this part of the proposed holiday tour. And without any false modesty, she knew she had coped pretty well. Even Marcus had been unable to find fault, although he hadn't actually praised her either, just given a couple of non-committal grunts. But then, his mood of the past couple of days had been fairly foul, he didn't take kindly to being a semi-invalid, even though it was only a very temporary condition.

The police hadn't found the thief who had burgled Marcus's room, then knocked him out, and Lacey knew it was very unlikely they ever would. He had disappeared into the teeming back streets of Kathmandu. A later check had shown that several small items were missing, cuff links, an electric shaver, a travelling alarm clock, and a few other easily portable things. Fortunately, most of their money and important papers had been in the hotel safe, and Lacey had been able to replace those stolen items which Marcus had needed.

But now they were back to the old stumbling-block again. Now that Marcus had been given a clean bill of health by the hospital, and since Lacey had dealt more than satisfactorily with all their business in Kathmandu, he planned to leave for Pokhara in the morning. And he was quite adamant that he didn't want her to go with him.

But Lacey was finding that she had unexpected reserves of stubbornness herself. She was slightly amazed that she actually had the nerve to defy him like this, especially since she knew perfectly well how fiercely he could react when people refused to fall in with his plans. The doctor's words kept echoing in her ears, though, and so she doggedly hung on, determined not to let him intimidate or override her.

'This trek certainly won't be a picnic,' Marcus warned, suddenly changing tack. 'There'll be a lot of miles to cover over some quite difficult ground, we might even end up sleeping rough some nights if we can't find anywhere to stay.'

Oh, so that was his new approach! she thought to herself a little grimly. The poor, helpless female won't be able to cope with the conditions, she'll fold up as soon as the going gets tough.

'There'll be a lot of women booking this holiday tour, once it's offered to the public,' she retaliated immediately. 'In fact, that's one more good reason for taking me along, to prove that a woman can cope with it quite easily.'

'Anyone booking this tour will be offered the option of taking the bus to Pokhara, instead of going on the trek,' Marcus reminded her.

'And you expect all the women to jump on the bus, while the men go striding off into the hills?' she challenged, with a fresh surge of indignation. 'If you think that's going to happen, you don't know the female sex very well!'

'To the contrary, I know them *too* well,' he retorted, scowling. 'And I certainly know how damned stubborn they can be. For the last time, Lacey, are you going to drop this plan to come with me?'

'No, I'm not. Not unless you can give me a perfectly valid reason why I should.'

He glared at her, frustrated. 'I thought we went through all this on the night we visited the temples. I gave you my reasons then, and none of them have changed.'

'Oh, come on,' she said, with a touch of scorn. 'Is that what this is all about? You think we're not going to be able to keep our hands off each other as soon as we leave Kathmandu? We're both adults, Marcus, we're quite capable of a little self-control.'

'All right, we've been skating around this for long enough,' he responded tersely. 'Perhaps it's time we brought the whole thing right out into the open.' His face darkened, and his grey eyes fixed on her with a sharp intensity that suddenly sent a deep shiver of unease through her. 'Do you want to know what the real problem is?' he challenged roughly. 'Then I'll tell you. But I don't think you're going to like it, Lacey. You see, you remind me of my ex-wife. I couldn't keep my hands off her, either. And I've absolutely no intention of getting caught up in that kind of situation ever again.'

His words seemed to whisk her breath away, her lungs suddenly felt so tight that they just wouldn't work.

'Oh, I don't mean there's a physical resemblance,' Marcus went on, slightly harshly. 'But I've started to react to you in exactly the same way. I look at you, and I want you. Just being in the same room as you is starting to drive me a little crazy. One reason I don't want you with me on this trip to Pokhara is that I don't want to end up feeling bloody frustrated twenty-four hours a day!'

Lacey gulped, her lungs shuddered, then they somehow started working again.

'You mean—you're still in love with your wife? Your ex-wife?' she shakily corrected herself.

A glint of grim humour showed briefly in the shadowed depths of his eyes. 'A romantic theory, Lacey—but wrong. That was the trouble, you see. I never did love her, I only wanted her. But I was pretty young then, I was too inexperienced to know the difference at the time. I've learnt a whole lot more about myself since, though. I'm good at sex, not at love.'

She swallowed hard. 'All right,' she said unsteadily, 'so you had a bad marriage. Something like that's bound to leave scars, I realise that. But it doesn't mean you can't cope with other relationships.'

Marcus stared at her in disbelief. 'Haven't you understood a single word I've said?' he demanded. 'My God, it's as if we're talking two different languages! Look, Lacey, for some reason you trigger off something inside me, and I don't like it, I don't want it to go any further. And I've already told you why, but I'll tell you again, I'll tell you a dozen times if that's what it takes to get through to you. The last time I met someone who had the same effect on me as you do, I married her. And do you know what that got me? Six months of heaven, and five years of sheer hell. There's no way I'm going to risk going through that again!'

Although there wasn't much colour left in Lacey's face, she wasn't ready to back down yet.

'So you made a mistake,' she said stubbornly. 'It's not the end of the world, it doesn't mean you've got to run away from women for the rest of your life.'

His grey eyes glittered brightly. 'Oh, I don't run away from them,' he assured her softly, and her skin prickled alarmingly at his husky tone of voice. Then his face darkened, his head came up and she flinched slightly at the new hardness of his features. 'But I like women who are interested in the same thing as I am: a casual physical relationship that can be ended at any time without tears or pain. Is that what you're looking for, Lacey?'

'No,' she whispered, with a small shiver.

'I didn't think so. But that's all that's on offer, as far as I'm concerned. It's been years since I've been capable of offering anyone anything else.'

'Have you even tried?' said Lacey in a very low voice.

'I don't need to,' Marcus answered flatly. 'I've got no illusions about myself, what I'm capable of. I know a great deal about sex, absolutely nothing about love. And that's something that isn't going to change.'

Lacey stared at him with troubled eyes. 'How can you be so sure about that?'

'Because I learn my lessons well. Only a fool would make a mistake like the one I made, then go and do the same thing all over again.' He gazed ahead of him broodingly. 'Do you know what made the whole thing so hard to take?' he muttered a few moments later, his tone slightly bitter now. 'It started off so well, and I thought it would go on like that for ever. I wasn't forced into the marriage, Clare didn't deliberately get pregnant or resort to any of those other tricks women sometimes use to get a man they want, I *wanted* to marry her. She was gorgeous, I couldn't keep my eyes or my hands off her, I simply wanted to be with her every hour of the day and night.'

Lacey wasn't at all sure that she wanted to hear any more of this, his words had started to trigger off a small, deep pain somewhere inside her, a growing ache which was stubbornly refusing to go away or be ignored. She didn't know what was causing it, she just knew that it somehow scared her, and she wanted him to stop talking before it got any worse. He seemed to need to unburden himself, though, as if it had all been locked away inside him for so long that he couldn't stop it pouring out, now he had finally unlocked the door and begun to open it a fraction.

'I was incredibly jealous, too,' he went on, his eyes very dark now, as if his gaze were fixed on something he didn't really want to see. 'I couldn't bear it if Clare even looked at another man, our social life was practically non-existent because I didn't want her to mix with other people, I just wanted to keep her all to myself. We seemed to spend most of our time in bed,' he admitted slightly huskily. 'We just couldn't get enough of each other. She only had to look at me and I'd ache for her. When she actually touched me, I went a little crazy. Our whole world revolved around the bedroom, I couldn't stay away from her, I used to wake up in the morning exhausted but still wanting her.'

Although she wanted to clap her hands over her ears, to shut out his hoarse confession, Lacey sat very still and didn't move. Part of her was absolutely numb with astonishment, she found it almost impossible to believe this was the same cool, controlled man she had worked for since last year. If someone had told her that Marcus Caradin was capable of behaving in such an irrational, obsessed way, she would have called them a liar.

'What happened?' she asked unsteadily at last, as the silence between them stretched on to the point where it made her nerves actually quiver.

'What happened?' he repeated with unexpected harshness. 'I'll tell you exactly what happened. I woke up one morning, and discovered that I didn't want her any more.'

Lacey stared at him with undisguised shock. 'But—it couldn't have happened just like that,' she stuttered. 'Not so suddenly. It *couldn't*!'

'I couldn't believe it either,' Marcus agreed, rather grimly. 'I lay beside her, I looked down at her, and I didn't feel anything except a hollow emptiness. I suppose what had happened was that I'd simply become satiated with her. We'd explored all the limits of physical pleasure together, tried all the different combinations we could think up, and suddenly there weren't any new discoveries to be made. The excitement, the novelty had somehow gone, the fire had simply burnt itself out. And it was then that I started to realise we didn't have anything to fall back on. Most physical relationships reach some sort of plateau. If you're in love, I guess it doesn't matter, just being together is enough. Without love——' he shrugged emptily, 'you're left with nothing.'

'How on earth did Clare take it?' whispered Lacey. 'She must have been completely shattered.'

Marcus's mouth twisted into a hard line. 'For a long while, she didn't even know. I didn't have the guts to come straight out and tell her that I just didn't want her any more. I tried to carry on as if nothing had happened, as if everything was exactly the same as it had been for those first few fantastic months. I wasn't any good at faking it, though. Oh, there were times when I still took her to bed. I was a very healthy twenty-five-year-old, and I've never been much good at celibacy. Making love to her just to meet a physical need made me feel so damned guilty, though, that in the end I got completely twisted up inside, I reached the point where I couldn't make it with her any more.'

'That must have been awful for her,' Lacey said, with a deep shudder.

'It was pretty grim for both of us,' Marcus agreed tensely. 'And once the physical side of our marriage finally ground to a halt, I realised how little we actually knew about each other. We'd been married only a few weeks after we met, I couldn't wait to tie her down in case she got away from me, met someone else. And for those first few months there hadn't been much chance for any serious talking, we'd been too obsessed with going to bed with each other. Suddenly, we had all the time in the world for conversation—and absolutely nothing to say. No common interests, no shared viewpoints—it was incredible, all that intimacy and yet we were like a couple of strangers.'

Lacey twisted her fingers together edgily. 'What did you do?' she asked in a strained voice.

Marcus stared directly at her, his glittering eyes for once completely readable. 'I'll tell you exactly what I did,' he told her, making no effort to hide his self-contempt. 'I did precisely nothing. As for Clare,' he gave a brief shrug, 'she eventually started to find her satisfaction elsewhere. I knew what was happening, but I didn't say anything, I didn't try to stop it. How could I, under the circumstances?'

'Why on earth didn't you get a divorce straight away? Why put yourself through all that torment?'

His gaze darkened. 'Because Clare didn't want a divorce,' he answered flatly. 'It was her way of punishing me for what I'd done to her. And I didn't think I had any right to push her into one. I'd already hurt her enough, I could hardly add insult to injury by forcibly cutting the legal ties, tossing her to one side like some novelty I'd suddenly grown tired of.'

'And you went on like that for *five* years?'

Marcus shrugged. 'For the first couple of years, I kept trying to put the broken pieces of our marriage back together again. I wouldn't accept that I couldn't work a miracle, that it couldn't be mended.' His mouth twisted harshly. 'Sheer arrogance, I suppose. But I'd never failed at anything before, and I found I didn't like it. At last though, I began to realise that we'd never really had a marriage. If I'd genuinely loved Clare, it couldn't have fallen apart so quickly. All there'd been between us was an explosion of physical attraction, so fierce that we'd been blinded to the fact that there wasn't anything else there, that there was no other point of communication between us.'

At that, Lacey's head snapped up indignantly. 'How do you know Clare didn't genuinely love you?' she challenged with sudden fierceness. 'All right, so *your* feelings were obviously pretty shallow, but it might have been very different for her.'

'I think that, in her own way, Clare loved me,' Marcus agreed. 'But once she'd got over the shock of discovering that I didn't want her any more, she never gave the impression of being exactly heartbroken. Looking back, I think she only clung on to our marriage for so long because she needed her revenge, her pound of flesh. She couldn't believe that I'd become sexually indifferent to her. It shattered her pride, she wanted to punish me for not wanting her, for making her feel less of a woman. And I wouldn't push her for a divorce because I could never throw off that damned sense of guilt. I always felt that I owed her, that she had the right to demand whatever she wanted from me.'

'But you did get divorced in the end,' Lacey reminded him in a quiet voice.

'Clare eventually met someone else she wanted to marry. He had more money than I did, and a minor title—quite a catch,' Marcus commented caustically. 'The divorce should have been quick and easy, but Clare always loved a touch of high drama, and the whole thing turned into a three-ring circus. Mud was slung, the lawyers had a field day, and the local press lapped it up. It cost me a small fortune—in both money and self-respect. By the time it was all over, I just wanted to get away. I sold out all my business interests and went abroad for a few months. I soon realised I wasn't cut out for a life of leisure, though, I needed to work, so I came back and started looking for a new challenge. I eventually heard of Worldwide Travel, and I knew it was exactly what I needed, a company on the verge of financial collapse where I'd have to work flat out in order to save it from going under. Work was what I needed to keep me going while I got my life back into some kind of order.' He looked up, and there were dark shadows in the depths of his eyes now. 'Then I had the bright idea of taking you with me on this trip to India and Nepal,' he growled. 'One morning at Varanasi, I took you down to the Ganges, put a marigold in your hair, and touched you. I couldn't believe it! It was like being with Clare all over again—at least, the way it was between us at the very beginning. I wanted you just as badly. If there had been a bed there, I'd probably have tossed you straight on to it. But I've had time to get my head together since, and I've made my mind up about one thing. I won't go through all that again—I simply can't face it.'

Lacey found she couldn't look at him. Her heart was beating in a weird way that was making her feel slightly dizzy, and she felt hot, confused, almost feverish.

'You don't know that it would be the same,' she muttered.

'No, I don't,' Marcus agreed tersely. 'But as long as there's the slightest chance, I'm going to do my damnedest not to get involved. Ever since the divorce, it's been the same. I can only cope with relationships where I'm totally in control. And I don't think I'm in control when I'm around you, Lacey,' he finished in a rough voice.

She shivered. 'We didn't have any problems when we were working together in the office.'

'That doesn't mean I was indifferent to you. Just that I found it much easier to keep it under control in a formal working environment. And you never gave the slightest sign of being interested in me. That helped.'

Her eyes were huge and dark now. 'If you felt like that, why on earth did you want me to come on this trip with you?'

He gave a small grunt of irritation. 'I told you, I thought I had it completely under control. If I'd had the slightest idea it would get out of hand like this——'

All at once, Lacey felt a violent surge of resentment towards Marcus, towards his stubborn refusal to put himself in a position where he could be hurt again. Her head shot up, and her green eyes blazed scornfully.

'Oh, yes, your famous self-control! Are you sure it's not your excuse for being a total coward, Marcus Caradin? All right, so you've had a rough ride over the last few years. But so have a lot of other people, and *they* don't end up running away from everything. What are you planning to do? Live the rest of your life in some kind of emotional vacuum?'

Marcus stared back at her angrily. 'If that's what it takes to keep my sanity, my self-respect—then yes, that's exactly what I'm going to do!' His face hardened. 'Not that it's any business whatsoever of yours.'

That last, totally unfair retort brought a sudden

prickling to the back of her eyes. Hurriedly wheeling round so that he wouldn't see them, she fumbled for the door-handle.

'There's not much point in talking about this any more,' she managed to get out, fighting hard to keep her voice steady. 'None of it really makes the slightest bit of difference. If you're mad enough to insist on going to Pokhara, then I haven't got any choice, I've got to follow the doctor's orders and go with you. And don't worry,' she went on, a note of sarcasm creeping into her tone now, 'your self-control might be at a low ebb, but there's nothing wrong with mine. If I can cope with Vittorio and all the other creeps like him, I shouldn't have any problems dealing with you!'

She heard his hiss of anger that she should even mention him in the same breath as Vittorio, but she didn't turn back, she just headed blindly for her own room, letting out a great sigh of relief when she finally reached it.

This was all getting completely out of control. How on earth was she going to get through the next few days? They would probably seem more like months!

Lacey slumped tiredly down into a chair. Well, this definitely settled one thing. Once they got back to England, she wouldn't have any choice, she would have to resign. Things had gone too far, there was no way she and Marcus were ever going to be able to get back to a formal working relationship. In fact, she would be heading home right now if it hadn't been for that wretched doctor and all his dire warnings about the danger of delayed concussion. And she knew Marcus too well to hope that he would cancel the trip. The damned man was too stubborn! Now he had announced to everyone he was going to Pokhara, nothing on this earth would make him change his mind.

She sighed deeply, and wished she could forget about the conversation they had just had. She was beginning to know and understand far more about Marcus than she wanted to. All the time she had worked for him, she had told herself he was the type of man her mother had always gone for, the type that she had always sworn she would never get involved with. It was beginning to look as if she might have been badly wrong about that, though. As he gradually stripped himself of his protective cover, he was slowly revealing himself as a man trapped by the past, haunted by old memories, and deeply disturbed by his own strong sexual drive. It was starting to make him seem almost vulnerable, and she didn't like that, it would be all too easy to respond to the tug of that vulnerability.

And she still kept doggedly telling herself that she didn't want that to happen. Just a few more days, she reminded herself tiredly, and then she would be free of him. She would make another new beginning for herself, find a job where she wouldn't be expected to go trailing through the wilds with a golden-haired man with soulless eyes.

Lacey gave a dark grimace, and fervently wished that the next week were already over.

CHAPTER SIX

WHEN Lacey woke up next morning, she just lay there for several minutes, reluctant to get out of bed and face the day ahead. Then she realised it wasn't the day she was reluctant to face—it was Marcus. She had to get it over with some time, though, so she finally hauled herself out from under the sheets, and made her way into the shower.

A quarter of an hour later, she very slowly made her way down to the dining-room, putting off for as long as possible the moment when she would meet Marcus again. Perhaps he would be sleeping late this morning, she told herself hopefully. Then she walked through the doorway and saw him sitting at the table. Her heart sank to practically ground-level, her pulses gave an odd little missed beat, then began to race rather erratically, and her legs felt uncomfortably weak as she went over to join him.

He glanced up as she sat down, and she was relieved to see his face was calm, his gaze quite impersonal, his manner brisk and businesslike. It was almost like having the old Marcus Caradin back again, the one she had worked for without any problems for the past year. And his first words confirmed his new attitude.

'I think the past few days—and particularly yesterday—are best put behind us and forgotten,' he said, his tone cool and efficient. 'We were both tired and at a low ebb, we said a lot of things we didn't mean. If you're

absolutely adamant about coming with me to
Pokhara——'

'Yes, I am,' Lacey cut in firmly.

'I thought you might be,' Marcus said drily. 'You
accused me of being stubborn, but my God, trying to
make you change your mind about something is about as
easy as trying to shift a mountain single-handed.'

'The doctor said——' Lacey began, but he held up one
hand in a gesture of defeat.

'I know perfectly well what the doctor said. According
to him, I'm not safe to be let out on my own, I need
someone to hold my hand every step of the way. The
man's well intentioned, but a fool—and a bloody
nuisance!' Marcus went on, with feeling. 'I'm not going
to argue about it any more, though, I just want to get the
rest of this job finished as quickly and as efficiently as
possible. So let's get this damned trek over with, tie up all
the loose ends, and get back to England as soon as we
can.'

'I'll go along with that,' Lacey agreed with some
fervour.

'Right, then,' said Marcus briskly, 'let's get down to
details. I sent one of the hotel porters out yesterday to buy
the extra items we'll need for the trek. We shouldn't need
to take too much with us. Some basic provisions, a couple
of changes of clothing, a medical kit in case of minor
accidents, a sleeping-bag each, and any small personal
items you might want to take. According to the people
I've spoken to, we shouldn't have any problems finding
somewhere to sleep at night, there are plenty of inns and
tea-houses scattered along the route. Treks like this are
beginning to get popular, and the Nepalese have
cottoned on to the fact that there's a good source of
income here if they provide food and shelter for walkers.'

'These supplies we're going to take with us—are we going to have to carry them ourselves?' asked Lacey without too much enthusiasm.

'They shouldn't be too heavy if we split them between two back-packs. If this trek works out well, though, and we eventually incorporate it into the tour, we'll probably have to hire porters for this stage of the holiday. Our clients probably wouldn't be too thrilled at the prospect of having to haul their own supplies across the Himalayas.'

'Can't *we* hire a porter?' suggested Lacey, glancing up at him hopefully.

Marcus's face remained implacable. 'You're a strong, healthy girl,' he told her firmly. 'And despite the opinion of the medical profession, I'm not going to collapse as soon as I'm put under a bit of strain. We should be able to manage the back-packs without any problems.' He glanced at his watch. 'How long will it take you to get ready?'

Lacey shrugged. 'Not long.' She was already wearing jeans, a cotton shirt, and sensible walking shoes. All she had to do was sort out the few things she would be taking with her, then pack away the rest of her belongings. The hotel would look after them until they arrived back in Kathmandu.

'Can you be ready in an hour? That's when the bus leaves.'

'Bus?' she echoed, briefly brightening up.

'It's only going to take us as far as the village of Dumre,' Marcus warned. 'That's where we'll be beginning the trek.'

'Oh,' she said, and gloomily concentrated on finishing her breakfast, her appetite only really perking up after Marcus had left to finish his own packing.

They were late arriving at the bus station, but it didn't matter, buses never left on time in Kathmandu. They found a couple of empty seats, then waited for several more minutes before the bus finally revved up noisily and roared off.

The journey to Dumre was an experience that Lacey very quickly decided she would have been more than willing to miss. The road was absolutely atrocious, pock-marked with so many bumps and potholes that every one of her bones ached ferociously from the constant jarring. She guessed that it wasn't doing much for Marcus's bruised head, either. And the road was so narrow that she couldn't even bear to think what would happen if anything came whizzing along in the opposite direction.

Then the road began to wind along the edge of a precipice, the bus trundling along so close to the perilously steep drop that Lacey actually groaned out loud at one point, then began to feel distinctly dizzy. A couple of minutes later, the driver started to get fairly excited. Taking his hands off the wheel in what Lacey considered to be a suicidal gesture, he kept pointing down to the valley floor far below them and shouting something which she couldn't quite catch above the grinding noise of the engine.

'What's he saying?' she asked Marcus slightly faintly, although she was fast reaching the point where she was past caring.

Marcus grinned unexpectedly, then directed her attention to the foot of the slope where, to her horror, she saw the crumpled wreckage of a bus that looked uncomfortably similiar to their own.

'Apparently, that was last Monday's bus,' he told her, his voice almost cheerful. And as she stared at him in appalled disbelief, he added placatingly, 'The driver said no one was hurt. By some miracle, they all escaped with just a few minor cuts and bruises.'

Lacey closed her eyes, then said weakly, 'How long before we reach Dumre?'

'Not long,' Marcus answered, sounding completely relaxed now. 'You're not worried, are you?'

'No, not worried. Just terrified! This is the sort of journey where you ought to make sure you write your will before you set out. How are you managing to stay so calm?'

'Perhaps some of the eastern sense of fatalism is beginning to rub off on me,' he said after a moment's consideration.

At that, her eyes shot open again. 'I don't believe that! You're not the type to just sit back and let things happen. Try telling me that you are, and I'll probably start to think that knock on the head's temporarily addled your brains.'

'I dare say you're right,' he agreed, with a faint smile. 'It's more likely that I'm looking at the whole thing from a very logical point of view. After all, what are the odds on two buses going over the edge in the same week? Pretty remote, I should think, even for Kathmandu's rather erratic transport system.'

'Why don't I find that more encouraging?' she muttered glumly. 'Well, in the case of a fatal accident, you'd better make sure my mother gets all my personal effects. She's the nearest relative I've got. In fact, just about my only relative,' she added a moment later. 'Except for a couple of great-aunts who disowned my mother years ago, and who avoid me like the plague in case my mother's over-generous nature turns out to be hereditary. How about you?' she chattered on nervously, finding that talking was helping to take her mind off the sheer precipice only feet away from the bus's threadbare tyres. 'Are you knee-deep in relatives, or do you have trouble scraping up enough for a family gathering?'

Marcus didn't answer straight away. Then he said, with obvious reluctance, 'I've just one sister, Ellen. She's a couple of years older than I am. Our parents died when we were very young, and soon after that Ellen was adopted, but they couldn't take the two of us so I was eventually fostered.' He gave a rather humourless smile. 'In fact, I got through several sets of foster parents. I suppose I wasn't a particularly easy child to look after. I still keep in touch with a couple of them, though, so perhaps their memories of me aren't all bad.'

'Perhaps that's why——' began Lacey slowly, then she abruptly shut up. She had been about to say that perhaps that was why he wasn't much good at relationships. If he hadn't had a chance to learn love as a child, what chance did he have now he was an adult? But she figured he was intelligent enough to have worked that out for himself, he certainly didn't need—or want—to hear it from her. And at the same time, she was fighting to suppress a deep ache of sympathy for him. He must have had a painfully lonely and unsettled childhood. She didn't want to start feeling sorry for him, though. Once she started off down that road, who knew where it would end? It could so easily open the floodgates to all sorts of inconvenient emotions, and she had already made up her mind not to let that happen, she was determined to remain as detached as he was.

'Is your sister married?' she asked, anxious to get back on to safe ground again.

'Yes, with a couple of nice kids, a boy and a girl.'

'You never had any children yourself?' That question had somehow popped out before she could stop it, and she immediately wished she hadn't asked it. Too late now, though.

Marcus was already frowning. 'No—thank God,' he said, a sharp note clearly detectable in his voice now. 'There's nothing worse than a divorce with some innocent child caught up in the middle of all the emotional rows and legal squabbling.'

Yet she thought she also caught a very faint hint of regret in his voice, as if it hadn't been his choice that there hadn't been any children. She decided it was time to get off this volatile subject, and she began talking instead about a couple of the business contracts she had negotiated in Kathmandu.

She was relieved—and slightly amazed—when they reached Dumre in one piece, the bus having suffered nothing more serious than a puncture which had been repaired with surprising speed. Both she and Marcus were hungry by this time, so they stopped for a meal of rice and lentils, Lacey's first introduction to the Nepalese staple diet.

'Pour the lentils over the rice, then eat it with your fingers,' advised Marcus. 'It's not very elegant, but it's certainly the most practical way of getting it into your mouth. And you'd better get used to the taste, you'll probably be eating a great deal of it during the next few days.'

To her relief, it didn't taste too bad at all. She finished the entire bowlful, then washed it down with sweet spiced tea. Marcus meanwhile pored over the map, and much to her relief he finally announced that they would stay the night in Dumre, then begin the trek in the morning. She suspected it wasn't concern for her aching bones that had prompted this decision, but the fact that the long, jolting journey had started his head aching ferociously again. He certainly looked worryingly pale, but she knew better than to comment on his pallor. Marcus clearly considered his state of health very much his own affair, and he wouldn't thank her for asking a lot of anxious questions.

They stayed the night in a small house that optimistically called itself the Krishna Hotel. Lacey had already done some background reading on the Nepalese way of life, so she wasn't too surprised to find she and Marcus were expected to share the upstairs room with the family's grandfather, who snored, a couple of young Nepalese children who giggled a lot, and two Austrian students who turned up at the last moment, desperate for somewhere to spend the night. The owner of the Krishna Hotel evidently didn't believe in turning away customers, so he dug out another couple of mattresses and squeezed the students into the already crowded room. They spoke hardly any English, but that didn't matter since Marcus spoke excellent German and Lacey had picked up a smattering of useful phrases during her mother's meandering trips around Europe. The two Nepalese children listened to their conversation with bright-eyed attention, obviously not understanding a word but enjoying it anyway, while their grandfather snored on peacefully, dead to the world.

The communal sleeping arrangements didn't bother Lacey. By the time she finally turned in, she was so tired that she simply closed her eyes and drifted off without any problems, not waking at all during the night. When she woke up the next morning, the two students had already left. They had told them the night before that they intended to make an early start. They were heading back to Kathmandu, then hiking on to India. Marcus had given a small grimace, and commented that it was fortunate not everyone wanted to travel independently, or Caradin Tours would have gone straight out of business.

After a breakfast of boiled eggs and more of the sweet spiced tea, Marcus decided it was time they moved off. Lacey stared a little suspiciously at his face, which still seemed to be a distinctly unhealthy colour. Despite all her resolutions not to interfere, she couldn't stop herself asking him if he felt all right.

'I'm fine,' he answered curtly, instantly looking annoyed. 'Don't try to mother me, Lacey! I won't stand for it.'

The thought of anyone attempting to mother Marcus Caradin made her eyebrows shoot up sky-high. Then her brows drew together in a light frown. It was obvious his relaxed mood of yesterday had completely vanished, this morning he was edgy and irritable, and she had the impression that he hadn't slept at all well last night.

'You've still got those pills the doctor prescribed for you,' she reminded him. 'Why not take a couple if you've got a headache?'

'I'm not taking any damned pills,' he growled back tersely. 'And if anything's giving me a headache, it's having to put up with a lot of prying personal questions.'

Biting back an equally rude retort, Lacey picked up her back-pack and manoeuvred it on to her shoulders. If he was feeling irritable because he wasn't feeling too good, it wasn't going to help if she kept on provoking him to the point where he finally exploded into a full blast of sheer bad temper.

The day turned out to be unexpectedly hot and humid, and as she trudged along behind Marcus, her legs began to feel increasingly leaden. The track they were following was winding its way gradually upwards, passing through paddy-fields that were bright green with growing rice, and past houses with tables set out in front, piled high with oranges, coconuts and papaya, which travellers could buy to quench their thirst.

Rather to Lacey's surprise, the track was fairly crowded. Most of the people they encountered were porters, bent low under loads of sugar and rice. His mood improving slightly as the day wore on, Marcus told her that their loads would be sold to villagers in the upper valleys. And coming the other way, the porters were carrying wood and woven goods, piled into wicker baskets which were carried on the tops of their shoulders, and held in place with a thick band which went around their foreheads. When Lacey worked out what those loaded baskets must weigh, she felt rather guilty about the way she had grumbled about the weight of her own comparatively lightly loaded back-pack.

The sun set in a blaze of colour that set the mountain peaks alight, and touched the valleys with muted shadows. As dusk set in, they finally reached the village for which they had been heading, and Marcus steered her towards a small house which was very similar in size and design to the Krishna Hotel in which they had stayed the previous night.

A little dazed now from tiredness, and her legs aching badly, Lacey stumbled through the door and found that the lower floor of the two-storey house was one large room which served as kitchen, dining-room and living accommodation. The small Nepalese woman who came bustling to meet them was dripping with jewellery: amber and jade necklaces, silver ear-rings, and a large gold disc through her nose. Her black hair was plaited with scarlet woollen braids, while the rest of her clothes were just as colourful, a scarlet shawl and bright green cummerbund over a black skirt and blouse.

'I'm beginning to feel distinctly under-dressed', Lacey murmured.

'Never mind about that,' Marcus answered briskly. 'Just put all those Nepali lessons you had with Mr Thapa to good use, and find out if she can provide us with a bed for the night.'

With the help of a phrase book and a lot of extravagant gestures, Lacey finally managed to make her understand that they wanted an evening meal, and to stay overnight. With a huge smile, their hostess herded them towards a table in the corner, then went back to the stove at the far end of the room from which tantalising aromas were already arising.

Lacey yawned. 'I think I'm too tired to eat,' she pronounced sleepily.

Marcus looked at her thoughtfully. 'Do you think we covered too much ground today? A lot of the people booking this holiday are going to be middle-aged or older. Would this kind of pace be too strenuous for them?'

'It might be a good idea to cut it down just a little,' Lacey said, after a few moments' consideration. 'On the other hand, if they were reasonably fit they would probably be able to cope. After all,' she went on pointedly, 'we've been carrying back-packs. That's bound to make us more tired. When our clients come on this holiday, they'll have porters to carry all their supplies.'

For the first time that day, a glint of amusement showed briefly in Marcus's grey gaze.

'If you really can't cope with the back-pack, perhaps we could hire a yak to carry the supplies the rest of the way,' he suggested smoothly.

'Could we——?' she began eagerly, then she saw the

open laughter in his eyes, and scowled. 'That's not very amusing!'

He didn't get a chance to reply because their hostess brought them their meal at that point, the familiar bowls of rice and lentils, accompanied this time by spiced cabbage and a saucer piled with tiny pieces of chicken. Lacey discovered that she definitely wasn't too tired to eat, and tucked in enthusiastically. When they had finished, their hostess came hurrying back and gestured towards a ladder that led to the upper floor.

'I think she's trying to tell us it's time to go to bed,' remarked Marcus, drily lifting one eyebrow.

'I wonder who's going to be sharing our bedroom tonight,' murmured Lacey in reply. 'Do you suppose every Nepalese house has its own resident snoring grandfather?'

But when they climbed the ladder to the large loft which comprised the upper floor, they found it completely empty except for two makeshift beds which had been made up in one corner. It was fairly obvious that their hostess wasn't expecting any more guests to turn up tonight, and that the loft was kept exclusively for visitors, it wasn't also a communal sleeping-quarters for members of their hostess's family.

She had given them an oil lamp to bring up with them, and Marcus set it down on the floor, then walked rather restlessly over to the far side of the loft. Lacey had the impression that he was suddenly very much on edge, and she wondered if his headache had begun to bother him again.

Finally, he swung back to face her, and she wished the flickering oil-lamp was throwing out a little more light because it was difficult to see him properly, to know what he was thinking—not that she had ever had much success trying to figure *that* out, she reminded herself wryly. All the same, there was enough light to see that his features were taut, his mouth set in an unexpectedly hard line.

'I don't think I can sleep here,' he announced at last, rather tersely.

Lacey glanced at him in surprise. 'Why not? The beds don't look too comfortable, I'll grant you that, but they're no worse than the ones we slept in last night. And we've got the sleeping-bags, we'll be all right once we're inside those.' She gave a faint grin. 'We'd better get used to roughing it, we're not likely to find many five-star hotels between here and Pokhara.'

He didn't smile back at her. If anything, his face seemed to have become even more grim.

'You're missing the point. When we set out on this trek, I wasn't counting on the fact that we'd have to share a room. At least,' he corrected himself, 'I thought if it happened, it would be very much the way it was last night, several of us packed in together, sharing what accommodation there was with other hikers and members of the Nepalese family we were staying with. I knew I could just about cope with that.'

Lacey deliberately misunderstood what he was saying. This trek was going to be difficult enough without digging up all their old problems again.

'So just for tonight we've got to share a room,' she said lightly. 'That's not going to cause any major difficulties, is it? I mean, I don't snore—at least, I don't think I do. And I certainly don't sleepwalk, so you won't have a disturbed night.'

His gaze was fixed intently on her now, though, and there wasn't a trace of any answering humour in it.

'Oh, but I *will* be disturbed,' he answered softly. 'Last

night was bad enough, I hardly slept at all.' His mouth twisted faintly. 'I somehow got through it, though—there wasn't much choice with all those other people around. But we're on our own now, Lacey. And things always seem to start falling apart when we're together like this.'

It was impossible to pretend any longer that she didn't know what he was talking about. Her pulses had begun to beat with that erratic rhythm that always affected them when he fixed that grey gaze on her so piercingly, and all her muscles were stiff with sudden tension.

'Look, if it'll make you feel any better, I'll sleep on the far side of the loft,' she offered in an unsteady voice.

'I don't think that'll make me feel any better at all,' he warned.

Lacey had the weirdest impression that the loft was starting to shrink, she was sure she was standing closer to Marcus than she had been before. Yet, at the same time, she knew that neither of them had moved an inch. Beginning to feel thoroughly unnerved, she bit her bottom lip nervously.

At the same time, Marcus slightly shifted his weight. The small but sudden movement made her jump, and as he saw her edgy reaction, he gave a low growl.

'This is ridiculous, we can't go on like this.' He turned round, and snatched up his sleeping-bag with a determined gesture.

Lacey stared at him numbly. 'What are you doing?'

'It's a warm night, I'll sleep outside,' he told her shortly. 'I'll be quite comfortable.'

Without thinking, she stepped forward and grabbed hold of his arm. 'That's crazy! You can't sleep out in the open——'

Her voice trailed away, and they both stared down at her fingers spread against his warm, tanned skin. Then

Marcus harshly knocked her hand away and stared down at her, his eyes blazing now with sudden fierce anger.

'What the hell do you think you're doing?'

Her ragged nerves abruptly flared out of control. 'Oh, I *do* apologise,' she shot back with furious sarcasm. 'I didn't know I wasn't allowed to touch you.'

His face darkened ominously. 'Don't play at being naïve, Lacey. You might be innocent, but you're certainly not stupid, you know exactly what's going on between us. Nothing's changed since that morning I first touched you, at Varanasi, I still want you, it never stops for a moment. I don't want to feel like this, my God, I certainly don't,' he confirmed savagely, 'but I can't stop it, I don't know *how* to stop it.'

Lacey gazed up at him, shaken; she felt totally out of her depth, she just didn't know how to deal with the situation. And she was a little terrified to discover that she wasn't at all sure she actually wanted to deal with it; something inside her was urging her to forget all about caution and common sense, pushing her slowly but surely towards the point where nothing mattered except giving this man exactly what he wanted.

She shook her head rather desperately. She had to get a grip on herself, it was sheer insanity to let this go any further.

'We were all right before,' she muttered in a low tone. 'We worked together for months without any problems. Perhaps we're just blowing this whole thing up out of all proportion——'

'What do you want? Tangible proof?' came Marcus's taut response. He caught hold of her wrist, pulled it forcefully towards him, only stopping when her hand was just inches away from his hard, erect body. 'Then just touch me, Lacey,' he challenged softly but urgently.

'That'll give you all the proof you're likely to need.'

Her hand seemed completely frozen, she couldn't move it a fraction one way or another. As the seconds ticked by explosively, the breath wheezed out of her constricted lungs and a hot ache began to grip the muscles in the pit of her stomach.

'Do you know what I want more than anything right now?' Marcus went on in a hoarse tone, staring straight into her dazed eyes, defying her to look away from him and knowing very well that she couldn't. 'I want to strip off your clothes, not slowly, but very fast because I can't wait to see you. Then I want to touch your breasts, lick your skin, touch and taste your sweetness.' Lacey quivered unrelentingly as his words washed over her, but he wouldn't release her, the sweet agony went on and on as his husky voice catalogued the extent of his need for her. 'When you're aching for me, as much as I ache for you, I want you to wrap your limbs around me, draw me down inside you, deeper and deeper,' he crooned softly. 'Then we'll be joined together so completely that we'll melt into each other, you'll be me and I'll be you, and we'll each feel exactly the same, we'll move together until the rhythm drives us both a little crazy, and the pleasure makes you want to shout out loud with sheer wonder and relief.'

His low tone mesmerised her, she swayed gently as the sensual images he had conjured up locked themselves into her brain, spinning her straight into a world she had never visited before. And it was strange, it was a world that had always frightened her a little, but she wasn't fearful any more, she wanted to go there so intensely that she actually gave a small shocked sound of longing.

Marcus's fingers were digging even deeper into her wrist now, but instead of pulling her closer, he had begun

slowly but forcefully to push her away from him, putting
a safe distance between them. And as her gaze stayed
locked dazedly on to his, she saw his eyes harden and
take on a coldly determined hue that made her shiver.

'But I'm going to fight tooth and nail to stop any of
those things happening,' he told her, his voice grating
harshly on her ears after the sensual undertones of only
seconds ago.

Lacey was finding it much harder than he was to drag
herself free of the spell. 'How do you know we can't make
it work between us?' she found herself whispering.

He lifted his shoulders in a brief, impatient movement.
'We've been over this before, I've already told you what
happens to the kind of desire we feel for one another
right now. It burns itself out. It's like lighting a fire, but
never putting on any more fuel to keep it going. Once the
fire's dead, there's absolutely nothing left. And believe
me, that's when you really feel the cold, it goes bone-
deep.'

'Are you absolutely certain that's what would happen
to us?'

Again, that swift shrug. 'I'm not a fortune-teller, I
can't see into the future,' he said abruptly. 'But as long as
there's the slightest chance, I'm not going to risk it. I've
been there before, and there's no way I want to go
through it all again. You called me a coward, and
perhaps I am, but that's just something you're going to
have to accept and I'm somehow going to have to live
with.'

He swung round, picked up his sleeping-bag again,
and without another word swung himself down the
ladder that led to the ground floor, swiftly disappearing
from sight.

Knowing that it would be useless to go running after

him—and not even sure that she wanted to—Lacey stood without moving for several minutes until her shivering body felt a little steadier. Then she walked over to one of the beds, spread out the remaining sleeping-bag, and slowly slid into it. Curling up in a small ball, she tried to close her mind to everything that had happened, but it wouldn't go away, it just kept hammering at her brain until, tired but still agitated, she forced herself to face it head-on.

The trouble was, she finally acknowledged to herself with a small shudder, Marcus insisted on looking at the whole thing from a deliberately simplified point of view. To go to bed, or not to go to bed. But she was beginning to get the uneasy feeling that it was starting to go much deeper than that; that was why they were both finding it increasingly difficult to cope with their turbulent reaction to each other.

What was the answer? She didn't know, she wasn't even sure there was one. Or what she wanted it to be.

Giving up trying to work it out, Lacey closed her eyes and tried hard to sleep. She finally managed it, but her dreams were so vivid and troubled that she ended up wishing she had stayed awake.

CHAPTER SEVEN

IN THE morning, Lacey reluctantly climbed down the ladder to the ground floor, and found that Marcus was sitting at the table where they had eaten their evening meal last night. Their hostess was already bustling around, preparing breakfast, and Lacey muttered a greeting before edging over to sit opposite Marcus.

She risked a quick glance at his face, then gave a faint frown. He looked—well, sort of distant, as if his mind was somewhere else completely. And his grey eyes weren't as sharp and alert as usual, they seemed almost unfocused, rather alarmingly vague.

A wave of deep anxiety ran through her as she remembered the doctor's grim warnings about delayed concussion. As they ate breakfast, though, boiled eggs and roti—a sort of unleavened bread—the usual crisp decisiveness gradually returned to Marcus's voice and manner, and Lacey let out a silent sigh of relief. It would be just too much if, on top of everything else, he became ill.

Once breakfast was over, they discussed the day's schedule and their planned route, but didn't once mention last night's near catastrophic encounter. In fact, they were unnaturally polite when they spoke to each other, and it soon became obvious that they were both being very careful not to touch on any topics that were even remotely personal. Lacey guessed that they had both reached the same conclusion—that they were only going to be able to survive the rest of this trek by staying distinctly cool towards each other. Neither of them wanted to get caught up in another emotional whirlpool like the one that had very nearly sucked them under last night.

During that day and the couple of days that followed, they slowly made their way through the valleys of the southern slopes of the Himalayas, following paths that led through paddy-fields and past villages surrounded by small plantations of banana plants and orange trees. And all the time they were very aware of the mountains that loomed in the background, their black and grey peaks soaring majestically up into a sky that, to Lacey's relief, remained cheerfully blue. She didn't think she could have coped with a downpour of rain; sodden feet and clothing would have been just about the last straw.

It was becoming clear to both of them that, as long as it was well organised, this trek should be well within the capabilities of most of the people who would be booking this holiday with Caradin Tours. Although the ground was often rough, there would be no problems as long as strong walking shoes were worn, and so far Lacey and Marcus hadn't had any trouble finding somewhere to stay each night, even though the food was proving a little monotonous. A basic diet of rice and lentils, even if it was sometimes dressed up with green vegetables, definitely began to pall after a while.

To their relief, they didn't run into any more difficulties concerning their sleeping arrangements. They always managed to find an inn that could provide a separate room for Marcus, although he usually had to share it with several members of the Nepalese family who owned the inn. He didn't seem to mind, though. In fact, Lacey had the clear impression that he would have slept outside with the goats rather than have risked sleeping anywhere near her.

She was still deeply worried, though, about his state of
health. Although he had told her he didn't believe in
taking pills, she had several times caught him surrepti-
tiously gulping down a couple of the white tablets the
doctor had prescribed for him. She guessed he must still
be getting fairly ferocious headaches, and he definitely
looked unnaturally white at times. More than that, she
was alarmed by the way his eyes sometimes took on an
unnervingly glazed look, very similar to the blank,
unfocused expression which had made her so anxious
that first morning. And he was irritable and preoccupied
for much of the time, as if he were struggling with some
problem that he refused to share with her.

She comforted herself with the thought that the main
part of the trek was behind them now, each day brought
them a little closer to Pokhara. From there, they would
be able to get a bus back to Kathmandu, where Marcus
could get medical help if he needed it, and she could fly
home to England—and sanity!

As dusk began slowly to close around them on their
sixth night out from Kathmandu, Lacey glanced up, then
gave a small frown as she realised there was still no sign
of the village where they had planned to spend the night.
In fact, now that she thought about it, she hadn't seen
any houses since early that morning, when they had
passed through a small village with a monastery that had
prayer flags fluttering above it, while a handful of yaks
grazed peacefully on the surrounding slopes. There were
no yaks in sight now, though. Nor any paddy-fields or
fruit trees—no sign of civilisation at all.

She stopped and turned to Marcus. 'Are we lost?' she
demanded bluntly.

Marcus studied the map, his brows drawing together

in a heavy frown. 'We must have taken a wrong path somewhere. Or perhaps the map's wrong. They warned me in Kathmandu that a lot of the maps of this area were inaccurate.'

Lacey stared gloomily up at the mountains which loomed all around them. Most of the time, she found them rather awesome, incredibly beautiful, and some-times a little unreal as they caught fire in the glow of sunrise or sunset, bathing themselves in magnificent colours. Now, though, for the first time they struck her as faintly menacing, cloaked in shadow and depressingly empty of all trace of human life.

'What are we going to do?'

'We'll keep going for a while longer,' Marcus decided swiftly. 'If we don't find the village in the next half-hour or so, though, we'll just have to find a sheltered spot and sleep rough.' It was very obvious from his tone of voice that he wasn't particularly pleased by that prospect. 'We're at a higher altitude now, so it'll be rather cold, but I don't see that we've got any alternative.'

Fervently hoping that at any moment they would see the pale shapes of white-walled houses looming out of the dusk, Lacey trotted after Marcus, not complaining about the fast pace he was setting because she was as anxious as he was to find somewhere relatively comfortable to spend the night. After a while, though, it became depressingly clear that they weren't going to find the village before full darkness set in.

Marcus reluctantly came to a halt. 'All right, we'd better make alternative plans. For a start, let's look for a spot that will give us a bit of shelter.' He glanced up. 'At least the sky's clear, it shouldn't rain. It could get pretty cold towards dawn, though, there might even be a touch of frost.'

'Whoopee,' commented Lacey glumly. 'I just love sleeping on cold, hard ground, then waking up covered with frost.'

His mouth hardened, and he seemed about to make a cutting reply. Then he visibly checked himself, and a second later he wheeled round, turning his back on her.

They were lucky enough to find a small hollow that was sheltered on one side by an outcrop of rock, and on the other by some low, stunted bushes. And there was the added advantage of a small stream splashing down the hillside quite near by, providing water for drinking and washing.

Lacey unrolled her sleeping-bag, then turned round just in time to catch Marcus swallowing another of those small white pills. Her brows wrinkled into a deep frown, and she just couldn't keep quiet any longer.

'Are you still getting bad headaches?'

'I'm fine,' Marcus answered curtly.

'Oh, sure!' she retorted. 'That's why you keep gulping down those pills every couple of hours.'

'I take three a day,' he growled back irritably. 'And sometimes not even that many. Anyway, what damned business is it of yours?'

'Oh, none,' she agreed, with more than a touch of sarcasm. 'Except that if you suddenly collapse on me, I'm the one who's going to have to find some way of getting you to Pokhara.'

His eyes glinted impatiently. 'I'm not going to collapse on you.'

Lacey's own temper began to stir. 'Can I have that in writing?' she demanded. Then her face altered, worry beginning to take the place of exasperation. 'Look,' she went on in a voice that suddenly sounded uncertain, even a little wobbly, 'we're stuck out here in the middle of nowhere, in fact we don't even know where we are right now. If something happens——' she swallowed hard, 'well, there isn't a doctor just around the corner, things could get—very difficult.'

'Don't get yourself into a panic,' Marcus told her, his own tone much quieter now. 'Nothing's going to happen, you're not going to find yourself in a situation you can't cope with.'

Lacey wasn't at all sure that she believed him. 'Then why do you keep taking all those pills?' she asked in a small voice.

It was quite a long while before he answered her. And when he did, he sounded oddly resigned and just a little bemused. 'Why do I always end up telling you things that I'd much rather keep private?'

She gave a rather helpless shrug. 'I don't know.' Then she looked at him worriedly. 'What do you want to tell me?'

He tapped his fingers together slowly, as if he was still reluctant to give her an answer. Finally, though, he lifted his head and said evenly, 'I *have* been getting an odd headache or two, but they haven't been too bad. And they're not the reason I've been taking those pills.'

'You mean there's something else wrong with you?' she asked, a fresh flare of anxiety making her go suddenly very cold.

Marcus briefly lifted his shoulders. 'I'm not physically ill, if that's what's bothering you. It's just——' he paused, then went on evenly, 'for the last few days, I've been getting these odd blanks in my memory.'

'Amnesia?' she squeaked in alarm.

'I suppose that's what you'd have to call it. But it comes and goes, sometimes I can remember quite a lot, sometimes hardly anything at all. For some reason, it's particularly bad first thing in the morning. A couple of mornings, I've got up and my mind's been almost a complete blank.'

Lacey stared at him in horror. 'I don't believe this! Do you mean to say you've been walking around these last few days with great holes in your memory? Why on earth didn't you tell me?'

'I didn't want to worry you. Anyway, as I said, it comes and goes. It's usually only really bad first thing in the morning. As soon as I'm up and on the move, most of it starts to come back again.'

She shook her head dazedly, she was still finding it hard to take in any of this. 'What can you remember right now?' she asked in a shaken voice.

'Practically everything that happened during my early life, right up to my twenties,' Marcus told her after a moment's hesitation. 'Then there's a rather big gap, several years seem to be completely missing. My memory really only picks up again at the point where I started up Caradin Tours. This last year's perfectly clear in my mind—at least,' he went on with a dark frown, 'it is up until these last couple of weeks. Then I start running into trouble again, there are several sizeable blank spots that I can't seem to fill in, no matter how hard I try.'

Lacey swallowed very hard, her throat suddenly painfully dry. The main part he had blocked out, that he apparently didn't want to remember at all, were the traumatic years of his marriage. She was no psychiatrist, but she guessed it had left a lot of deeply etched scars that refused to heal. He had already admitted that he didn't like to fail, and there was no doubt that his marriage had turned into a disaster that had severely dented his male pride, his self-esteem, the very roots of his confidence. If the concussion was making his memory play tricks on him, then that was definitely one part of his life he would want to blank out. But he had just admitted he was also having problems remembering what had happened these last couple of weeks.

'Amnesia's usually only very temporary,' she got out at last. 'It'll probably put itself right in a few days.'

'That's what I keep telling myself,' he agreed, rather wryly. 'But so far there doesn't seem to have been very much improvement.' He looked at her thoughtfully. 'I don't know why, but I get the feeling you could fill in quite a few of those big gaps in my memory, if I asked you to. Did I tell you very much about myself?'

She stared at him uneasily. 'You don't remember anything about the conversations we had?'

'Sometimes I think that I do,' he answered, with a touch of frustration, 'but it's always just out of reach, I can't quite remember any of the details, all the key bits seem to be missing—and they're the bits that'll make sense of all the chaos inside my head.' His gaze fixed on her with sudden intensity. 'Do you know what's eating away at me most of all right now? It's that I can't sort out my relationship with *you*. Oh, I know that you work for me, but I get the feeling it goes further than that. All the relevant pieces of memory have somehow got lost, though, and I'm going damned near crazy trying to get them back again so that I can figure out what the hell's going on, how I'm supposed to act towards you.'

Lacey found she was actually shaking now. No wonder Marcus had been so fiercely irritable and distracted over the past few days. He must have felt he was going slowly out of his mind as great chunks of memory kept slipping away from him.

'I don't think it's much good my telling you what you want to know,' she decided at last, her voice still unsteady. 'It's probably best if you try and remember it for yourself.'

'But how long's that going to take?' he demanded with a fresh burst of frustration. 'And what am I supposed to do in the meantime?'

'Damn it, I don't know!' she flung back at him, equally sharply. Her nerves were so raw and ragged that they were starting to affect her temper now. Then she somehow got control of herself again. It wasn't going to help him if they ended up having a flaming row. 'Look, in just a couple more days we'll be at Pokhara,' she went on placatingly. 'Just hang on until then, and you'll be able to get some proper medical help. The doctors will sort out your amnesia in no time at all.'

'First of all, we've got to *get* to Pokhara,' Marcus reminded her a little grimly. 'Right now we're lost, remember? For all I know, we could be wandering round in circles.'

'Yes, we could,' she retorted edgily. 'But that's not my fault, *you* were the one doing the map-reading.'

To her astonishment, the dark frown left his face and he suddenly grinned. 'I might be having a few problems working out what kind of relationship there is between us, but one thing's pretty obvious. You're not scared of me, are you? And I like that.'

'Have all the other women in your life been scared of you, then?' Lacey retaliated, his unexpected change of mood throwing her even further off balance and making her frazzled nerves jangle even more badly.

'Some of them seem to have found me a little— intimidating,' he told her smoothly. 'And not many of them stood up to me.'

She could well believe that! Then something else struck her. 'You can *remember* all those other women?'

The corners of his mouth twitched slightly. 'You make it sound as if there were dozens of them,' he replied drily. 'Although it probably isn't doing my reputation much good, I have to admit the numbers were very much smaller than that. And yes, I can remember them. So why am I having all these problems remembering the important things concerning you, Lacey?' he went on, in a suddenly husky tone of voice. 'For example, I can very clearly recall which of those women I took to bed. And what happened there.' Lacey was very glad it was growing dark because she knew she had started to blush fiercely. 'But have I been to bed with you?' Marcus challenged softly. 'Somehow, I don't think so. I don't know for certain, of course, but I can't help thinking I wouldn't have forgotten it, if I had.'

Her face was positively glowing now. 'I'm your secretary, that's all,' she told him stiffly. 'We've got a good working relationship, but that's as far as it goes.'

He nodded slowly. 'Perhaps,' he agreed, obviously not completely convinced. 'But my instincts are telling me something quite different. Anyway, it doesn't really matter. Eventually, I'm going to fill in all those missing gaps, then I'll know precisely where I stand with you.'

Lacey forced herself to look away from him. What good would it do for him to remember? she reminded herself, with a trace of bitterness. All he would find out was that he had already decisively vetoed any close relationship between them, that he was absolutely adamant that he didn't want to get involved with her.

Should she tell him, get things straightened out between them right now? Then her shoulders slumped. What would be the point? He would remember for himself soon enough, his memory was sure to come flooding back in just a few days. And in the mean time, it would probably be best not to push it. She seemed to remember reading somewhere that amnesiacs shouldn't be forced to remember things, that it was best to let the lost memories come filtering back in their own good time. And it wasn't as if he had forgotten absolutely everything. Just the important parts, she reminded herself a little tensely, the personal traumas that his strained mind had apparently decided it didn't want to think about right now.

'We'd better get settled down for the night,' she mumbled, suddenly not wanting to discuss the whole difficult subject any more tonight.

Marcus looked at her piercingly, as if trying to see right inside her head and read all the mixed-up thoughts tumbling around in there. Then, to her relief, he simply nodded and seemed perfectly content to drop the subject for now.

They managed to scrape up a basic evening meal out of the supplies they were carrying, and after they had eaten, they wriggled into their sleeping-bags, still fully dressed for extra warmth as the evening had begun to grow more chilly. Lacey was certain that Marcus fell asleep almost immediately, he lay very still, and his breathing was quiet and even. There was no way she could sleep, though, not after the bombshell with which he had hit her earlier. What if his amnesia got worse? What if he woke up in the morning and found he couldn't remember her at all?

Oh hell, what a mess it all was! she told herself frustratedly. And what if it turned out they had wandered right off the beaten track, that they had got themselves completely and hopelessly lost, with nowhere to turn for help in an emergency?

She gave a small shiver of pure fear, then deliberately

closed her mind to that possibility. If she kept thinking
along those lines, she would only end up driving herself
crazy. She had to start thinking positively, telling herself
that Marcus's memory would steadily improve, that they
would soon reach Pokhara, that in no time she would be
back in England and this whole nightmarish trip would
finally be over.

Tossing restlessly, Lacey realised she was hot and
flushed, despite the fact that the night had turned quite
cool. Her face felt as if it were burning, her clothes were
sticking damply to her body, the sleeping-bag was
beginning to feel like a straitjacket.

Slowly and quietly, she unzipped it, then carefully got
to her feet. There was just enough moonlight to let her see
her surroundings. Moving silently, she crossed the
clearing, then groped her way towards the small stream
that ran down the hillside just a few yards from their
temporary campsite.

She located it more by sound than by sight, the quiet
gurgling of the water carrying clearly on the still night
air. Dropping down to her knees, she splashed the ice-
cold water against her overheated face, rinsed her hands
and wrists, and felt her body temperature slowly return to
normal.

Lacey wasn't quite sure how long she sat there
afterwards, just soaking up the peace and quiet, staring
up at the peaks that soared up into the night sky. The
peaks shimmered palely as the snow-caps reflected the
moonlight, while the dark bulk of the lower slopes was
striped with different shades of black as the shadows
gathered thickly in hollows, then thinned out again on
the open stretches. Feeling a new sense of calmness, a
fresh determination to cope with whatever the next
couple of days had to throw at her, she eventually got up

and began to make her way back to the campsite.

She had nearly reached it when a heavy patch of cloud drifted over the moon, completely obscuring it. Immediately, the darkness became almost impenetrable; without that pale light she could hardly see her hand in front of her face. Feeling her way along, she let out a tiny grunt of relief when she realised she was finally back at the clearing. Bending down, she began to grope around, trying to find her sleeping-bag, but it was several minutes before she finally located it. She slid her fingers along the edge, searching for the unzipped opening, but then she let out a gasp of pure shock as she felt a hard, warm shape beneath the down-filled nylon.

'Wrong sleeping-bag,' came Marcus's quiet murmur out of the darkness. Then a faintly challenging note entered his voice. 'Or was it a deliberate mistake, Lacey?'

'It certainly wasn't!' she shot back instantly. 'It was just so dark, I couldn't see.'

'Well, now you're here——' he said, softly but meaningfully. While she was still trying to work out what he was up to, he closed his fingers around her wrist, then gave a gentle but swift jerk, pulling her completely off balance. An instant later, she went tumbling down on top of him, and for a moment she was blindingly aware of her body crushing against his hard outline. He gave a small grunt that sounded like a mixture of a gasp and a chuckle, then he remarked ruefully, 'I think you've just bruised a fairly vital part of my anatomy!'

'Sorry,' she mumbled automatically. Then her head shot up. 'No, I'm *not* sorry,' she said furiously. 'It was entirely your own fault.'

'You're probably right,' agreed Marcus. Then he went on, slightly mockingly, 'I suppose it wouldn't be much use asking you to rub it better?'

The colour surged into her face because she was getting to know his voice only too well, she was uncomfortably aware that he was only half joking, that a part of him actually ached for her to do precisely that.

'I'd better be getting back to my own sleeping-bag,' she said stiffly.

His fingers didn't relax their grip on her wrist. 'In just a moment. First of all, I want you to try and explain something to me.'

'What?' she asked, very warily. She wished it wasn't so dark, this would be easier to deal with if she could only see his face, know exactly what he was thinking right at this moment. Then she remembered how good he was at disguising his feelings, she probably wouldn't be able to guess what was going on in that complicated mind of his even if there were a blazing electric light directly overhead.

'Just now, when you first touched me, an odd picture flashed into my mind,' Marcus told her slowly. 'I could see you standing in front of me with a bright orange marigold in your hair. The petals seemed to glow against the red of your hair, and I had the feeling that it was—well, somehow significant.'

Lacey felt her skin prickle almost painfully. 'Why—why should you think that?' she stuttered.

He was silent for a moment, then finally shrugged. 'I don't know. I thought that perhaps *you* could explain it to *me*.'

'Well, I can't,' she said flatly.

'Can't—or won't?'

His question briefly threw her. 'Let's just say that it wouldn't make any difference in the long run,' she got out at last. And she knew she was absolutely right about that.

Once he got his memory back, he would remember all about the marigold, and what had happened between them that morning on the bank of the Ganges. But by then he would remember all the rest of it, too, which meant they would be right back to square one again, with them both backing away from each other, determined not to get involved.

But that didn't solve the problem she was facing right now. And she was beginning to realise it definitely *was* a problem—and not just from his point of view. It was getting harder all the time to remember that she hadn't wanted any involvement, either, that right from the beginning she had been determined to keep their relationship on a formal footing.

Well, this certainly wasn't very formal, she told herself slightly desperately. Lying on top of him in his sleeping-bag, feeling his fingers locked disturbingly firmly around her wrists, knowing somewhere deep inside her that she really didn't want him to let go——

He shifted position a fraction, so that she found herself wedged even more comfortably against him.

'It's strange how everything can seem so different at night,' he remarked, almost conversationally. 'One of my foster parents used to tell me it's because the demons come out after dark, and they pop all sorts of devilish thoughts into our heads.'

'You must have had very strange foster parents,' she replied rather breathlessly.

'That particular one certainly had a very vivid imagination,' he agreed. 'But perhaps he was right about the demons. Would you like to know what's going on inside my head right now, Lacey?' he challenged huskily.

'No, I don't think so,' she said very hurriedly.

Although she couldn't see his face clearly in the

darkness, she was sure he was smiling. 'I think I'll tell you anyway. Those demons are whispering in my ear, putting all sorts of highly unsuitable ideas into my mind. And the trouble is, I'm starting to listen to them, something inside me's beginning to say, why not, just this once?'

Lacey's eyes opened very wide, for a moment she couldn't believe he had actually said that awful phrase again. 'Just this once.' Then she realised that he had no recollection of saying it that first time. He couldn't remember how it had immediately turned her off, how she hadn't been able to hear anything after that except Vittorio's voice saying exactly the same thing, hadn't been able to feel anything except that rat's hands crawling all over her.

Yet for some reason, the same thing wasn't happening this time. It was strange, but that short phrase seemed to have lost its power to conjure up the old memories that had so sickened and disgusted her. The only voice she could hear right now was Marcus's, and he certainly didn't turn her off. Quite the opposite in fact, she was alarmed to find a warm ache pleasantly spreading through her body, it was almost as if she were starting a fever. Only this fever wasn't the sort that ran its course and then went away, she told herself a little desperately; this type of fever could last a whole lifetime. That was why it would be much safer not to catch it in the first place.

But Marcus was still holding her wrists, and she had the uneasy feeling that he had absolutely no intention of letting go of her. And her own will-power seemed to have sunk to a dangerously low ebb. When he pulled her even closer, she found it hard to put up more than a token resistance and she was certain that he knew it, that he was even rather pleased by it. Her head started to feel oddly woozy, there was a curious sense of inevitability about what was happening.

His fingers drifted slowly, almost casually, to her blouse, the buttons slid apart with ease, and she found herself suddenly remembering what he had said to her at that inn, just a few nights ago. 'I want to strip off your clothes, not slowly, but very fast, because I can't wait to see you.' But he wasn't moving fast, in fact his hands were drifting along in a controlled, almost leisurely manner.

Then she realised that it was probably because it was so dark that he was managing to keep things moving at such a slow pace. He couldn't see what he was touching, and that was somehow helping him to hang on to his self-control, to take pleasure in a gentle exploration instead of hungrily grabbing what he wanted.

Which meant that she had plenty of time to stop him— if she wanted to. Her head jerked up. Of *course* she wanted to, she told herself firmly. But she still couldn't actually do anything about it, all her muscles had gone curiously limp and lethargic, it was so hard to move, to speak, even to think.

'Very nice,' Marcus murmured a little thickly, as his fingertips drifted appreciatively over the upper swell of her breasts. Then he encountered the light cotton barrier of her bra. 'But I think we can do without this,' he went on, and she meant to protest, but didn't, and then it was too late, the bra was undone, tossed aside, and she was left naked to the waist. Yet it was odd, she didn't feel in the least self-conscious or embarrassed. The darkness covered her, she couldn't see her own half-naked body, she could only feel a warm, sweet, spreading pleasure as Marcus's fingers continued on their subtle journey of exploration.

He lingered for a long time over the outer curves of her breasts, as if deliberately prolonging the delicious tension that was beginning to build up between them. Then, without warning, his hand slid inwards, his palm brushed the hard central peak, and she was slightly appalled to hear herself groaning out loud as exquisite sensations shot through her in the wake of that brief, gentle touch.

His fingers took the place of his palm, rotating slowly, stirring up all the new, wild feelings to a fresh pitch which left her gasping. If he can do this with just his hand, she thought to herself in near panic, what on earth will it be like if he touches me with the rest of his body? And she found herself shuddering in anticipation, the breath was tremulously expelled from her tight throat.

Marcus was still playing with her nipple, squeezing it lightly between his fingertips now, as if it were a new but already much-loved possession.

'I know exactly what it looks like, even though I can't see it,' he told her huskily. 'Small and virginal and dark pink. Am I right, Lacey?' he breathed against her ear.

'Yes,' she somehow managed to get out in a strangled voice, and she heard him give a small grunt of satisfaction. But the touch of his hands wasn't quite so leisurely any more, they were moving down slightly restlessly over her stomach, tugging a little impatiently at the belt of her jeans. Without even thinking what she was doing, she moved her hips, making it easier for him. He found the fastening, slid down the zip, and at the same moment his mouth came down over hers, as if he was determined to stifle any protests she might have been going to make. But the thought hadn't even crossed her mind, she was lost now and she knew it. As his mouth intimately caressed hers, probing deep into its warm sweetness, she instinctively opened up to him, her hands began to tug at him, pulling him closer, while her long legs rubbed restlessly at the rough denim of his own jeans.

His answering response, blatantly obvious, sent a deep thrill spiralling through her, she was aware of a surging sense of triumph, she couldn't remember ever feeling anything like it in her life before. And all of a sudden, *she* was the impatient one, deeply resentful of the barrier of clothes between them, giving a muffled moan of protest because the hard pressure of his body was driving her a little crazy. Marcus heard her moan, he moved still closer, his weight gently crushing her, his body sliding against hers in a slow, rhythmic caress, setting up an excruciatingly pleasurable friction that left her gasping. She knew his self-control had reached a dangerously low level, but she didn't care; in a blaze of self-knowledge she realised this was what she had been waiting for, longing for, since the moment when he had first touched her, at Varanasi. It was useless to pretend any longer she didn't want to get involved, she *was* involved, and it was marvellous, her whole body seemed to be singing with sheer delight.

The moon slid out from behind its covering of cloud, and the clearing was bathed in its silvery light, she could see the pale glitter of Marcus's hair now, the shadowy outline of his face. And she knew that he could see her, spread out beneath him as she waited impatiently for his touch, her hair loose and tousled, her eyes feverishly bright with the riotous new emotions he had set free inside her.

And she had thought that being able to see each other would make it even better, make it perfect. But somehow it wasn't working out that way, she slowly realised that

Marcus had gone very still, he hardly seemed to be breathing now, and she could sense a deep tension beginning to build up inside him.

'What—what is it?' she whispered in a shaky, uncertain voice.

He stared down at her. 'Something inside my head just said "no",' he told her roughly. Then his mouth set into a grim, humourless smile. 'It's one hell of a time for my mind to start playing tricks on me! But that "no" was very loud, very definite.' He shook his head in sudden frustration. 'What does it mean, Lacey?'

But she couldn't answer him straight away, she had started to feel cold, she knew in just a moment she was actually going to shiver. Despite his loss of memory, something deep inside him had still thrown up all the old barriers at the very last moment. His determination not to get involved with her was implanted in him so strongly that it had even broken through his temporary amnesia. He didn't know *why* he shouldn't be touching her, he was just following a basic instinct that was too deep-rooted and powerful to be ignored.

Marcus growled impatiently, then gave her a brief shake. 'Come on, Lacey, I need an explanation. And right now!' he instructed harshly. 'I'm going a little crazy wanting you, but there's a voice inside my head yelling out no, telling me I shouldn't be laying a finger on you. Why am I getting all these messages? Tell me, damn it!'

Gazing up at him with shocked eyes, she tried to find the right words. 'It's all rather complicated.'

'Then make it simple!' He shifted his weight away from her, gave a brief mutter of angry frustration, and deliberately dragged his gaze away from the pale gleam of her skin. 'Let's get a few things straight about the way our relationship developed after we arrived in India. Did

I want to take you to bed?'

Ridiculously, she felt herself flushing. 'Yes, you did,' she muttered.

'But I didn't, did I?' His mouth briefly relaxed into a wry twist. 'I might only be able to remember brief snatches of everything that's happened these last few days, but for some reason I'm absolutely certain I'm right about that. So you'd better tell me *why* we didn't have an affair.'

Quite suddenly, though, Lacey had had enough. She felt cold, empty, totally humiliated, and she definitely wasn't up to an intense cross-examination at the moment. She struggled awkwardly back into her clothes, then swung back and glared at him.

'Why didn't we have an affair?' she challenged, fighting to keep the raw pain out of her voice. 'Do you really want to know? It was because you were too much of a coward, Marcus! You've had some bad experiences in the past, and you decided you didn't want to risk going through anything like that again, so you backed away from any kind of emotional relationship. You haven't got the guts to take on any new commitments.' Seeing the angry disbelief beginning to glitter in his eyes, she rushed on. 'Oh, I'm telling you the truth all right. I don't suppose you like it, but you'll get your memory back again soon enough, and then you'll know I'm not lying!'

She ran over to her own sleeping-bag, wriggled inside it, then deliberately turned her back on him. For several tense minutes, she waited to see if he would say something, do something to deny the accusations she had flung at him. There wasn't a sound, though; she got the impression he was sitting absolutely still, not looking at her but staring into the distance with those soulless eyes of his.

Her own eyes felt hot and sore now, and even though she closed them, they kept prickling and watering. It was the cold, she told herself stubbornly, the night air was getting quite chilly. She definitely wasn't crying, no one in their right mind would waste tears over someone like Marcus Caradin.

She quietly blew her nose, wiped her damp cheeks, then braced herself to face the depressing, sleepless night that she knew stretched ahead of her.

CHAPTER EIGHT

THE hours of darkness seemed to last for ever. Lacey actually sighed out loud with relief when the first glow of dawn finally began to lighten the black velvet of the sky. Rather gingerly, she moved. Her body felt stiff and seemed to ache inside, and she wasn't at all sure it was solely the result of having to spend the night lying on the cold, hard ground.

A few minutes later, she reluctantly rolled over, and the first thing she saw was Marcus's silhouette, and the pale glitter of his golden hair. He was sitting with his arms loosely wrapped around his drawn-up knees, and from the brooding expression on his face she had the distinct impression that he was wishing he were anywhere except right here.

He must have caught her movement out of the corner of his eye because a few moments later he turned his head and looked at her.

'Did you sleep well?' he asked politely.

Lacey stared at him in amazement. Was he joking? But another glance at his shadowed face was enough to convince her that he was hardly in the mood for jokes.

'Not particularly,' she answered at last, deciding it would be best to stick to the truth. 'How's your memory this morning?'

'Patchy,' came his curt response.

Her glance flickered back to him edgily. Did that mean he couldn't remember last night? He intercepted her gaze, and instantly interpreted it correctly.

'Don't worry,' he assured her a trifle grimly, 'I can remember the last few hours very clearly indeed. I wish that I *could* have forgotten them, I might have slept rather better last night.'

'We'll reach Pokhara fairly soon,' Lacey said, trying hard to keep her voice light and steady. 'Everything will be all right then. All we've got to do is try and stick it out for the next day or so, until we finally get there.'

'And what will happen then?' enquired Marcus, with cutting sarcasm. 'Will there be a little man with a magic wand? He'll just wave it, and put everything right again?'

'I just meant——' Lacey suddenly dropped her shoulders, defeated. 'I meant that we won't have to be under each other's feet all day long, the way we are now. The trip will be more or less over, we can fly back home, things can get back to normal again.' She raised her head and looked at him directly. 'That's what you want, isn't it?'

'I suppose so,' muttered Marcus. Then he shook his head impatiently. 'I won't know for certain until I can *remember* what I want.' For an instant, he looked blazingly angry and frustrated. Then he made an obvious effort to get himself back under control again. 'You're right, we've just got to get through the next couple of days as best we can. It's no use chasing this thing round and round in circles, or we'll both end up a little crazy. Let's get this trek over with, finish the job we came here to do, and try to forget about personal problems for a while.'

He made it sound so easy, Lacey told herself with a painful grimace. But he was right, there really wasn't any alternative. They weren't going to get anywhere by talking it over for hours and hours. The sensible thing— the only thing—they could do was somehow close their minds to everything except purely practical problems.

'All right,' she said a few moments later, trying hard to force everything else out of her mind. 'How about some breakfast?'

A flicker of incredulity showed in his grey eyes. 'You're hungry?' he said disbelievingly.

No, she wasn't. In fact, she wasn't at all sure she could even face the sight of food at the moment. But she was trying very hard to pretend everything was normal, and she thought it was about time he made an effort to do the same.

The same thing seemed to occur to him because, without another word, he got up and began to go through his back-pack, sorting out the last of their food supplies. Then he deftly built up a small fire so that they could heat up some water for coffee.

His appetite seemed as poor as hers when it came to actually eating breakfast, but since they had very little food left anyway, they managed to get through most of it. Marcus drank a cup of coffee, then gave a slightly bleak shrug.

'Apart from the coffee, that's the last of our supplies gone. Short of trapping a yak, it'll be some time before our next square meal.'

His poor attempt at humour didn't raise an answering smile from Lacey. Instead, she glanced around with deep gloom. 'You won't find any yaks around here,' she predicted. 'They've got more sense than to wander into a desolate spot like this.' She was ready to admit that it had a certain grandeur, a wildness that might have appealed to her at any other time, but she just wasn't in the mood to appreciate it right now.

As soon as breakfast was finished and the fire carefully doused, they set off in what Lacey fervently hoped was the direction of Pokhara. She had great faith in Marcus's map-reading ability, she was sure he was as competent at that as he was at everything else. But that competence wasn't much use if the map was inaccurate to begin with.

They walked on steadily through the morning, and by lunch time Lacey was beginning to get tired, rather hungry, and more than a little alarmed. They had walked all this way without seeing any sign of human life. What if they were wandering further and further away from the beaten track, into some really wild and uninhabited part of Nepal?

'Surely we should have come across a village by now?' she questioned rather anxiously.

'Not necessarily,' Marcus told her. 'Quite a few of these valleys are uninhabited, they're simply not fertile enough to grow rice or support livestock.'

'You're so good at cheering me up,' she muttered. She was puffing rather breathlessly now, struggling to keep up with the fast pace he was setting. 'Will you slow down a little?' she demanded a few minutes later, glaring at his retreating back. 'My legs are just about to drop off, and all you keep doing is going faster and faster.'

He seemed on the point of making an equally irritable reply. Instead, though, his face altered and he came to an unexpected halt.

'If you're tired, we'll take a short break. I don't suppose it'll hurt to rest for quarter of an hour.'

Lacey immediately felt guilty because she knew he was worried by the prospect of having to spend another night in the open, with no food and virtually no chance of getting any. It was why he was pushing on at such a killing pace, hoping they would stumble across a farm or village before night set in.

She sighed softly and hitched her back-pack more comfortably on to her shoulders. 'I'm all right,' she said

resignedly. 'I suppose we'd better push on——' Her voice
trailed away as she suddenly screwed her eyes up and
squinted into the distance. 'Am I imagining things?' she
said slowly, a few seconds later. 'Or is that smoke?'

Marcus turned round and gripped her arm. 'Where?'
he asked intently, not seeming to realise that his fingers
were digging quite painfully into her skin.

The touch of his hand momentarily threw her, she
couldn't answer him straight away. 'Over there,' she
finally managed to croak out slightly unsteadily, pointing
towards the far end of the valley.

It *was* smoke, a thin curl of it drifting lazily up into the
air.

'I can't see any houses,' frowned Marcus.

'Well, there's got to be someone there,' Lacey
answered practically. 'Fires don't simply light
themselves.'

'We'd better go and take a look,' came his decisive
response. Almost before he had finished speaking, he
had released her arm and headed off in that direction,
leaving Lacey to trudge along behind him, rubbing her
skin where he had gripped it and wishing it would stop
tingling quite so disturbingly.

It took them half an hour to track down the source of
the smoke. When they did, they both stood still for
several moments, just staring at the sight which
confronted them.

There was a hut, but it was practically a ruin; just a
couple of tumble-down walls and a small section of the
roof still remained. Its derelict state didn't seem to
trouble its sole occupant, though. Sitting cross-legged in
the tiny patch of shade afforded by the roof sat an elderly
man with the most tranquil face Lacey had ever seen, his
skin as brown and wrinkled as old, cracked leather.

Although it was fairly warm, he was wearing a robe trimmed with wolf fur, a wolf-fur hat, and thick boots, and he was staring contentedly into the distance while a fire crackled noisily near by, heating up a couple of pots which obviously held his dinner.

With just a touch of nervousness, Lacey took a couple of steps forward.

'Namaste,' she greeted him.

The old man didn't seem in the least surprised to see them. It was almost as if he had been expecting a golden-haired man and a red-haired girl to drop in while he was indulging in half an hour's quiet meditation before dinner.

'Namaste saathi,' he returned her greeting comfortably. Then a flood of Nepali followed, but Lacey couldn't understand more than a couple of words.

'I'm not sure, but I think he's inviting us to join him for dinner,' she said, turning back to Marcus.

'Then let's take him up on that offer before he changes his mind,' Marcus answered promptly. 'I'm so hungry, I could eat just about anything.'

Lacey haltingly thanked the old man, and as they went over to join him, she took the opportunity to glance into the two pots that were heating up over the fire.

'It's rice and lentils!' she muttered. 'Oh Marcus, I know it's generous of him to share his meal with us and I'm grateful, I really am. But when we get back home, I don't ever want to see another lentil or grain of rice!'

But when the old man finally dished up the meal, she ate hungrily, and felt much more cheerful afterwards. Marcus put down his own empty bowl, and turned to her. 'Ask him if he knows how to get to Pokhara,' he instructed.

Lacey raised one eyebrow. 'You've got great faith in

my command of Nepali,' she remarked drily. 'I told you,
I never got much further than yes, no and thank you.' But
she dug the battered phrase book out of her back pocket,
pored over it for several minutes, and then finally tried
out a few stumbling words. As soon as he heard her
mangled version of his language, a huge grin spread over
the old man's face. Lacey grimaced. 'I think we've just
given him his first good laugh of the day.'

'Try again,' Marcus urged.

After a lot of false starts, the old man finally seemed to
get the gist of what she was trying to say, and he launched
into a spate of directions which seemed to consist mainly
of pointing south-west several times with great vigour.

'I think I get the message,' said Marcus, expressively
lifting one eyebrow. 'We go that way?' he queried,
pointing his own finger south-westwards. The old man's
head nodded up and down with enthusiasm, then he
started chattering on again.

Lacey gave a small groan, and grabbed the phrase-
book. 'I wish he'd speak a bit slower, I'm only catching
about one word in twenty. What's a *goth*?' she muttered
under her breath. 'Oh, here it is. A shepherd's hut.' She
glanced up at Marcus. 'I think he's trying to tell us there's
a hut up ahead where we can spend the night—if we ever
manage to find it,' she added rather pessimistically.

Marcus looked at his watch. 'There's still three or four
hours of daylight left. We'd better push on while we can.'

They said goodbye to the old man, then left him sitting
cross-legged by the dying embers of his fire, placidly
gazing into the distance.

Lacey glanced back at him one last time. 'What's he
doing out here, all by himself?'

'He's probably a hermit,' Marcus answered.

Her brows drew together in a worried frown. 'Will he

be all right, out here on his own?'

He shot her a slightly exasperated glance. 'If anyone's going to end up in trouble, it won't be that old man. He's lived in these mountains all his life, he's perfectly well equipped to survive here—which is more than can be said for us!'

Reluctantly conceding that he was right, Lacey trudged on. Not long afterwards, they stumbled across a faint trail, and Marcus decided they might as well follow it since it seemed to be heading in the direction the old man had pointed out.

It wound steadily upwards until the muscles in Lacey's legs began to screech out in protest. And it was getting chillier, too, a light breeze was swirling down the valley and sending goose-pimples chasing across her skin.

'Are you sure we're going the right way?' she demanded, when they stopped for a few minutes to get their breath back. 'I can't see any hut.'

'Do you want to walk back to that old man and check the directions with him?' enquired Marcus irritably, and Lacey bit back an equally sarcastic retort because she realised his uncertain temper was only caused by anxiety. Things were beginning to look pretty bad. The light was already fading, the wind was gathering in strength, and there still wasn't any sign of the hut.

She didn't protest when he set off at an even faster pace. The path wound its way past a sprawling clump of rhododendrons, then Marcus abruptly stopped and she cannoned straight into him.

'Hey, what——?' she began indignantly, then she shut up because her gaze had just fixed on what he had already seen. A small hut, half hidden behind the rhododendrons and tucked snugly into the hillside.

It was very basic and rather dilapidated, but right at

that moment it looked like a palace to Lacey. Even when
they opened the door and found it was virtually bare
inside, she wasn't dismayed. At least they would be out of
the chilly wind, and she could finally rest her aching legs.
And by the time Marcus had spread the sleeping-bags on
the raised area at one end and lit a couple of candles from
their small stock of emergency supplies, it looked almost
cosy.

Lacey settled herself on one of the sleeping-bags,
massaged her aching feet, then glanced up at Marcus.
'I'm rather thirsty,' she said rather apologetically. 'I don't
suppose we've got anything to drink?'

Marcus shook his head. 'No, sorry.' Then he looked
thoughtful. 'These huts are usually built fairly near to a
small stream, so any occupants have got a regular water
supply. I'll go and take a look, see what I can find.'

'I'll come with you,' she said quickly, jumping to her
feet. She definitely didn't fancy being left here on her
own.

'There's no point, I'll only be gone a few minutes. Stay
here in the warm.' He left before she had the chance to
argue with him, and once he had gone, the hut suddenly
didn't seem so safe and cosy any more. Even the candles
didn't seem to be giving off quite so much light.

Lacey scrambled over to the window, unlatched the
shutter, and nervously peered out. It was dark outside
now, though, the newly risen moon was still low in the
sky, and she could hardly see a thing. Her eyes very
slowly adjusted to the darkness, then her pulses gave an
optimistic thump. Wasn't that something moving around
just beyond the rhododendrons? Marcus must have
found the stream, and already be heading back to the
hut.

And yet, somehow it looked too small for Marcus. Oh

damn, if only it weren't so dark, she muttered to herself edgily. She screwed up her eyes and peered out again. Then her brows drew together in a deep, nervous frown. It was crazy, she knew she had to be wrong, but that shadow *looked* like——

Then, just for an instant, she was absolutely certain she could see narrow eyes glinting fiercely in the darkness. Giving a terrified yell, she rushed to the door, flinging it open just as Marcus appeared on the other side.

'What the hell——?' he got out, as she flung herself straight at him.

'There—there was something out there,' she gabbled. 'It was—oh, Marcus, don't laugh at me, but I'm sure it was a wolf!'

To her astonishment, he didn't bat an eyelid.

'It probably was,' he agreed calmly, and without the slightest trace of concern.

She stared at him in disbelief. 'It *was*? Well, what are you going to do about it?'

His grey eyes took on a slightly amused hue. 'What exactly would you like me to do? Wrestle it single-handed?'

'No, of course not,' she muttered, beginning to get the glimmering of a suspicion that she was making a fool of herself. 'But isn't it dangerous?' she pressed on with a rush of fresh anxiety. 'It's got to be dangerous!'

'Not if we leave it alone,' Marcus told her patiently. 'I'd say its chances of getting through that door were fairly remote, wouldn't you?'

Lacey stared at the thick wooden door to the hut, then slowly but very grudgingly nodded her head. 'I suppose so,' she conceded.

'Then perhaps you'd stop trying to strangle me,' Marcus suggested. Highly embarrassed now, she hurriedly disentangled her arms from around his neck.

'I wasn't really worried about me, I was worried about *you*,' she admitted in a low voice. 'You were all alone out there in the darkness, I could picture the wolves creeping up on you, pouncing on you——' She gave a deep shiver as her vivid imagination supplied all the gory details.

'It was only one wolf, not a pack,' Marcus pointed out. 'And it was probably just doing the same thing I was, looking for water. By the way, I found the stream,' he went on. 'Are you still thirsty?'

'No!' she said at once. There was no way she would let him go out into that frightening darkness again.

She wrapped her arms around herself, it was quite warm inside the hut, but somehow she couldn't stop shivering. It wasn't just the heart-stopping appearance of the wolf, it was the tensions and strains of the last few days all starting to crowd in on her at once. Her whole body had begun to shake quite relentlessly, and she couldn't stop it.

'Cold?' questioned Marcus sharply.

'I don't know,' she muttered uncertainly, and it was true, quite suddenly she didn't know what she was feeling.

Marcus seemed to hesitate for a moment, then he finally reached out and enclosed her icy hands in his own. Briskly, he began to rub them, skin brushing against skin until the steady friction finally began to produce a faint glow of heat.

'Better?'

'I think so,' Lacey managed to get out in a voice that had started to quaver alarmingly. Then she gave a nervous laugh. 'I think you'd have to rub me from head to toe, though, to get me really warm.'

Marcus abruptly let go of her. 'It's an interesting

theory,' he said, his features suddenly taut. 'But in practice, it would probably have fairly disastrous consequences.'

'That depends on what you consider to be a disaster,' Lacey babbled, her tongue showing an alarming tendency to run away from her.

She heard him draw in a quick, rather unsteady breath. 'Stop it, Lacey,' he warned, a little grimly. 'Remember what I told you about the demons? They're starting to whisper in my ear again, and I can't control those whispers at night as easily as I can during the day.'

But she was feeling curiously light-headed now, for some reason it didn't seem to matter what she said. Anyway, perhaps it was time he heard a few home truths. She lifted her head and stared up at him a little dizzily. 'Do you know what the trouble is with you, Marcus Caradin? It's that you've got too *much* damned control. And that can be dangerous, it can lead to all sorts of problems. High blood-pressure, ulcers, stress illnesses—heart problems.'

'There's nothing wrong with my heart.' His grey eyes darkened perceptibly. 'The problem right now is in a very different part of me,' he added drily. 'But I can cope with that—as long as you don't push me.' Then he stared at her shrewdly. 'What's the matter, Lacey? Right at this moment, you look like the one who's under stress, not me.'

She ran her fingers shakily through her hair. 'I don't *know* what the matter is,' she admitted unsteadily. 'All I know is that it's getting to be impossible to cope with the way things are between us.' She somehow managed a wry grimace. 'Do you know why I enjoyed working for you? It was because it was a nice, steady job, no great upheavals, no major surprises. I turned up at the office every morning, worked hard through the day, then went home in the evening to my comfortable flat. I really enjoyed the regular routine. After all those years of living with my mother, trying to cope with her muddled, messy life-style, it was fantastic to have my life mapped out so neatly. Then you dragged me off on this trip, and ever since then nothing's been the same, everything's somehow got turned upside down.'

Marcus lifted one eyebrow reflectively. 'So why am I getting the impression you've enjoyed almost every minute of it?'

Lacey glared back at him indignantly. 'I most certainly haven't!' she denied. 'I told you, I liked the way my life was working out, everything was going exactly the way I'd planned it.'

'I suppose the novelty of a settled life-style hadn't quite worn off yet,' Marcus conceded. 'But a few more months, and you'd have started to get bored out of your mind.'

'How do you know that?' she demanded.

He shrugged. 'You're too young, too bright, too intelligent to tie yourself down to a routine office job, then go home every evening and sit in front of the television like some middle-aged matron.'

'Who are you to lecture me?' Lacey retorted instantly. 'After all, *your* life isn't exactly smooth-running, is it? Or do you think it's healthy to live like some kind of monk?'

His face instantly darkened, warning her that she was straying on to dangerous ground again. She didn't care, though; there was something about this isolated hut, the pressing darkness outside and the glow of light and warmth within its thick walls that made intimate conversation seem almost too easy, the words just kept pouring out of her.

'I don't live like a monk,' Marcus denied, staring hard

at her now. 'I've already told you that.'

'Oh, no,' she agreed, with a touch of scorn. 'You don't mind getting involved in a relationship as long as you stay totally in control.'

His brows drew together in a brooding frown. 'This is pointless. We're starting to talk about something that I can't even remember properly.'

Lacey stared back at him challengingly. 'And I told you *why* you can't remember it. You've blotted it from your mind because you can't face the fact that you're a coward where personal relationships are concerned!'

'I don't have to take that from you,' he began furiously, his eyes glittering with a flare of pure anger.

'Well, you'd better take it from someone,' she cut in, slightly amazed at her own recklessness. 'Or you could well spend the rest of your life with great gaps in your memory.'

She expected him to retaliate with a biting blast of temper. Instead, though, he didn't say anything at all, and after a while she began to find his silence disturbing. A dark flush had spread over her face now, she was beginning to realise she had gone too far, and she fervently wished she had kept her mouth shut. He had called her intelligent, but she was bleakly aware that it wasn't very clever to start an argument in a place like this, where they were cooped up together and couldn't get away from each other.

Chewing her bottom lip nervously, she wondered if she should apologise. She glanced edgily at Marcus; then her gaze swung back to him and this time stayed fixed on him with a deep rush of unease.

She was getting to know his face so well; it wasn't hard for her to read the signs clearly written there. The new darkness of his eyes, the faint spread of colour along his cheekbones, the set of his mouth—he had forced back that fierce surge of temper, but all that explosive emotion had had to go somewhere, and it had started to divert itself into other channels, still gathering strength, still potent—and far more dangerous.

He shifted a fraction closer, and she instinctively shrank back as his shadow fell over her, the dark silhouette of his body outlined by the flickering candlelight.

'Let's get back to basics,' he suggested softly. 'Do you want to cure all my problems, Lacey? Is that what this is all about? But I've only got *one* problem right now.'

She tried to speak, but the words just wouldn't come out, they were somehow all locked up inside her confused, whirling head. Instead, she stared numbly up into his eyes; she couldn't remember ever seeing them quite so dark before, not grey but nearly black, and hot and haunted.

'I was trying to remember how all this started,' he went on huskily. 'Then I remembered the demons. And how you felt cold. They're still whispering in my ear,' he told her, his gaze never leaving her face for an instant. 'And you've started shivering again. It looks as if we've come full circle, Lacey.'

'That's all we do,' she muttered. 'Keep going round and round in circles.'

'Then perhaps it's time we tried to break the chain.' And she had the clear impression that it wouldn't matter if she agreed with him or not, they had already gone way past the point where it would make the slightest difference.

He took hold of one of her hands again, folding her icy fingers within his own for a few seconds, then he began rubbing them slowly. Yet it wasn't quite the same as

before; this time there was a subtle rhythm to his
movements, and he didn't stop when her fingers were
warm and tingling, but just kept moving, working his
way gradually along her wrist, then her forearm, leaving
swirling patterns of pleasure rippling over her skin.

If ever there was a time to pull back, it was now, Lacey
told herself shakily. And yet somehow she couldn't do it;
as soon as he had touched her, something inside her had
seemed to fall to pieces, leaving her feeling defenceless
and frighteningly vulnerable. Nor did Marcus seem to
have much more control over the situation than she did;
his hands were already sliding across and undoing the top
buttons of her blouse. A muffled, half-hearted protest
sounded in her throat, but he ignored it, his head was
already bent, his golden hair brushing against her
burning skin as first his mouth, then his tongue, explored
the exposed skin of her throat.

'I think you're beginning to warm up, Lacey,' he
murmured unsteadily. 'Soon you'll be as hot as I am.'

His hands moved relentlessly onwards, and only
seconds later her blouse swung open, letting him bury his
hands in the soft flesh underneath, a grunt of deep
satisfaction escaping him as he pressed even closer. His
fingers weren't still for a moment, they kept exploring
further and further, as if they were greedy to discover all
the other treasures that lay in wait for them. Then
somehow her bra had gone, his head was at her breast,
his tongue licking hotly, moistly, as if she tasted of pure
nectar. And she wasn't protesting any more, in fact the
sounds coming out of her throat were quite incomprehen-
sible, tiny sobs, then a small, choked gasp of pure
pleasure as his fingers stroked and gently squeezed, and
the lethal lashing of his tongue reduced her to a melting,
almost animal-like delight.

Then Marcus's own shirt was somehow undone, she hadn't the slightest idea which of them finally removed it, but at last his supple skin was exposed to her searching fingers, she murmured appreciatively as her palms rubbed over its warm, golden smoothness. Dipping into the valleys below his ribs, rising over the smooth line of his back, lingering lovingly over the strong outline of his shoulder-blades, she revelled in the tactile contact, and was hungry for more.

Briefly lifting his head, Marcus stood very still for a few seconds, his breathing quick and even. 'Very nice, Lacey,' he told her at last, his voice little more than a husky whisper in her ear. 'But it's not enough. Not this time.'

A small quiver of nervousness ran through her as he gently but firmly pushed her down on to the sleeping-bags, and her stomach muscles actually trembled as she stared up at him, saw the bright flush running over his cheekbones, the fierce, feverish glint in his eyes as he gazed down at the perfection of her half-naked body.

'I know it's probably not a good idea,' he muttered thickly, 'in fact, it's just about the craziest thing we could do right now. But I think I've got to, Lacey. I really think I've got to.'

Her breath was wheezing in her throat now, she couldn't get out a single word, but somehow it didn't matter. And her nervousness of only moments ago had somehow miraculously vanished, she wasn't scared of the unknown, or even apprehensive about her own ability to please. This wasn't a competition, there weren't any points to be scored for experience and expertise. The only important things were loving and wanting and giving, and she could do all of those, they were so simple, so marvellously, incredibly easy——

Lifting one hand, she brushed it lightly against his moist skin. 'I think I love you, Marcus Caradin,' she heard herself murmuring, to her own astonishment.

A dark frown briefly shadowed his face. 'Don't say that,' he instructed a little roughly. 'Don't spoil it.'

But Lacey simply smiled up at him. All right, she wouldn't say it. But he couldn't stop her thinking it. And she had the feeling he might even eventually get used to the idea, he hadn't actually been angry. In fact, his eyes had gleamed very brightly for an instant, before he had swiftly clamped down and refused to let himself respond.

But he was responding now in a very different way, stripping off her jeans and pants, then impatiently removing the last of his own clothes. His fingers instantly returned to caress the achingly sensitive peaks and hollows of her body, and she could feel the need growing in him to a near-explosive pitch. Yet underneath the fierce rush of desire, she could also sense a new carefulness; somehow he was managing to hold back a fraction longer than he had probably thought himself capable of only moments ago. And with a rush of surprise and gratitude, she realised that he was resolutely determined that she should keep pace with him, that he was refusing to let himself race ahead of her even though the effort was half killing him.

And that forceful self-control was already reaping the results he had intended. As his hands and tongue moved in skilful unison, glorious waves of pleasure surged over her from head to toe, rolling down through her breasts, lodging between her thighs, whispering against her silken inner skin.

Marcus paused, and Lacey closed her eyes, instinctively tuning in to the hard, beating pulse of his body. Something inside her seemed to be throbbing in an identical rhythm, and she moved restlessly, rubbing against him, silently begging him to show her the next steps in this dance of love.

And he was only too willing, his weight briefly crushed her, and she instantly locked herself around him, as if frightened he would pull away from her at the very last moment. But there was no chance of that, her hot closeness had already burned away what little will-power he had left, and she heard herself cry out loud with relief as the first powerful, uncontrolled thrust of his body took away some of the ache that had started to consume her.

A small part of her had been expecting pain, and she was willing and ready to face it, but it was over so swiftly that she hardly noticed it. In an instant, it was buried deep under a great wall of pleasure that hit her, nearly flattened her. And then a brand-new ache started up inside her, far more intense than anything she had experienced so far. Their bodies quickly found the intimate shared rhythm they had sensed in each other before, and Marcus's movements became quick and strong, yet unexpectedly gentle, as if beneath all that pent-up desire there was still the iron determination not to hurt her, to make it as good for her as it was for him.

And it *was* good, unbelievably good, she could hardly believe it could get any better. But then something exploded inside her, and the world seemed to disintegrate into tiny fragments of excruciating pleasure that pierced every corner of her body. And at the same time, Marcus groaned out loud, his body stiffening, then shuddering convulsively as he fiercely plunged into his own tumultuous climax.

For a long time afterwards, she seemed to drift in a delicious limbo, dazed, incredibly happy, her body boneless and totally languid. She had just enough energy for a faint murmur of protest as Marcus at last slid his body from hers.

He propped himself up on one elbow, then gazed down at her. 'Don't be greedy,' he told her, with a grin. 'You don't appreciate something if you're allowed to have it all the time. By the way,' he went on in the same lazy, relaxed tone, 'I forgot to kiss you.'

Lacey stared at him blankly; she had the distinct impression that he had kissed just about every inch of her—including some places that made her blush bright red just to think about them.

His grin widened as he saw the surge of colour spreading across her skin. 'Oh, yes,' he agreed, 'I kissed your breasts, your stomach, your thighs, and quite a few other very delicious parts of you. But somehow that didn't leave time to kiss your mouth. We've plenty of time now, though,' he added meaningfully, and before she had a chance to say anything, he had bent his head and she found herself drifting away on a brand new wave of pleasure as he slowly and very thoroughly explored every corner of her mouth.

When he finally raised his head again, Lacey sighed in pure contentment. 'Do you remember the nickname everyone's given you at Caradin Tours? "Miracle Man",' she reminded him, a hint of laughter brightening her eyes. 'I wonder what they'd say if they knew about the miracles you can perform when you really put your mind to it,' she went on a little dreamily.

Marcus traced one finger lightly over the swell of her breast, watching with some satisfaction as the pink tip instantly responded to his touch. 'On the contrary,' he observed softly, 'I think that when it comes down to it, you're the one who's pulling all the miracles out of a hat.'

'Me?' she echoed, looking up at him in some surprise.

He shifted a little closer, then grinned again, rather wickedly this time, at the expression on her face as she discovered he was already fully aroused again. 'You see?' he teased huskily. 'All I ought to be capable of right now is a goodnight kiss. But look—a miracle!'

Lacey fluttered her eyelashes at him in wide-eyed innocence. 'Good heavens. What on earth do you suppose we ought to do about it?'

His slate-grey eyes abruptly altered to a very different, much darker hue as he subtly changed position.

'I'll show you *exactly* what to do about it,' he assured her, in a voice that was suddenly thick and hotly urgent.

And she was eager enough, but she didn't think it could possibly be the same as it had been last time. And it wasn't. It was better! Deliciously slow, every pleasure-filled moment was stretched out to almost unbearable limits until she felt her body would simply break up beneath him.

Afterwards, she lay motionless for a long time just gazing at Marcus in pure awe. Then eventually they both slept, slipping easily into the deep, relaxing sleep of physical exhaustion.

When Lacey finally woke up again, daylight was filtering into the hut, and she was rather stiff from lying on their makeshift bed. But then she became aware of other, fainter aches scattered around her body, and her eyes shot open as she remembered exactly what had happened last night. Then her face became slightly troubled. How was Marcus going to react this morning? He had been fighting against this relationship so fiercely, so stubbornly, but it had finally happened anyway, neither of them had seemed able to do anything to stop it. So how was he going to take it? And where was he?

She slowly sat up. The bed was empty; so was the hut.

The door was slightly ajar, though, so she guessed he was somewhere outside. A quick shiver ran over her, and she realised a cool draft of early morning air was drifting over her bare skin. Forcing her languid body into action, she got up and started to dress.

She had just pulled on her jeans and zipped them up when the door opened and Marcus came back into the hut. For several seconds, she couldn't do anything except simply stare at him. His face was already completely familiar, the cool grey eyes, the perfect bone structure, the hard yet sensual line of his mouth, and the bright gold hair. Yet with a deep inner quiver, she realised that the rest of this man was now familiar to her, too; she knew every intimate inch of him, knew what he looked like— felt like——

With an enormous effort, she stopped her mind going any further. There wasn't any point, she already knew that this morning was going to be very different from last night. *He* was different. She had sensed it the instant he had walked into the hut. A fresh surge of apprehension spread through her already tense muscles, and the remembered pleasure of last night began to retreat to the very back of her mind.

Marcus was looking directly at her now, a slightly brooding expression darkening his features. 'Are you— all right?' he asked, rather abruptly.

'Fine,' she answered, making a determined effort to keep her voice brisk and light. 'What did you expect? To find me wailing and beating my breast because I'd lost my virtue?'

'Stop it, Lacey!' he ordered sharply. Then he lifted his shoulders in a frustrated gesture. 'There's not much point in keeping the truth from you. I've got my memory back. I woke up this morning, and everything was crystal clear in my mind. I can remember every detail—my marriage, my ex-wife—why I didn't want to get involved with you——'

Lacey tried hard to convince herself she was pleased that he was cured, that the amnesia had been swept away so quickly and completely. But it was hard to be overjoyed, because where did that leave her? Not in any place she particularly wanted to be, if the closed expression on his face was anything to go by.

'So where do we go from here?' she asked rather unsteadily, at last.

'I don't know,' Marcus growled. He moved restlessly, then swung back to face her again. 'Last night was fantastic,' he told her, in a carefully controlled voice. 'But it shouldn't have happened. It was all my fault, I accept that. I was the one who let things get out of control. And now I don't know what the hell I can do about it.'

She felt the resentment beginning to bubble up inside her, but she somehow forced it back. 'I don't see that there's much either of us has got to do,' she told him stiffly. 'We can just leave things as they are. After all, the message is coming across loud and clear. Last night was fun, but it was a mistake and now it's over. Have I got it right?'

She had no idea how she was managing to keep so cool, so outwardly controlled. What she really wanted was to rant and scream, to throw herself at him and physically kick and bite, get her own back for the way he was so callously tearing her apart. Instead, though, she just stood there, her limbs frozen, talking to him in this funny voice that really didn't sound at all like her own.

Marcus prowled away from her again, going over to stand in the doorway, as if instinctively seeking an escape route.

'Put like that, you make me sound like a prize bastard,' he muttered in a low, angry tone. 'Perhaps I *am*. But I warned you what I was like, what I could cope with—and what I couldn't.'

'And you can't cope with me?' she challenged, the first note of bitterness creeping into her voice.

'No, I don't think I can,' came his harsh response. 'At least, not right now. I don't *want* it to be like this——'

'Don't you?' she cut in with sudden hard scorn. 'But perhaps you do, Marcus. Perhaps all you really want is straight sex, with no complications, so you use your failed marriage as an excuse for not getting involved in any relationship that'll demand more of you.'

He glared at her furiously. 'No one talks to me like that!'

'Don't they? Well, I do!' she retorted. 'I think that last night gives me the right, don't you?'

He strode forward and gripped her arm, his face so blazingly angry that she was sure he was going to shake her until he had forced her to take back her accusation. But then both of them froze because it was still there, they could feel it throbbing between them, the torrent of physical and emotional response that had thrown them together last night, that had been haunting them ever since that morning at Varanasi. For a few fraught seconds, they simply stared at each other, shocked and appalled that their bodies could betray them like this.

Marcus was the first to move. With an obvious effort, he let go of her and stepped back, his face set and pale.

'Let's get packed and get out of here,' he said abruptly.

Minutes later, they were ready to leave. Neither of them had said another word, and when they left the hut, Lacey didn't once look back but just grimly stumbled after Marcus as he set off at a furiously fast pace.

She had been wrong last night, she told herself in a choked voice. There hadn't been any miracles after all. Just a few hours of blissful pleasure, that were now going to have to be paid for with weeks, months, perhaps even years of pain and regret.

CHAPTER NINE

By LATE morning they had reached the next valley, which was far less bleak than the one they had just left behind. Green paddy-fields patterned the valley floor and the lower slopes of the mountains, and half an hour later they sighted a small village.

After that, it was unexpectedly easy. They bartered their sleeping-bags in exchange for a ride in an incredibly ancient truck to Pokhara, stayed overnight in a hotel, then next morning caught the bus that would take them back to Kathmandu.

Conversation between them seemed to have hit an all-time low. The few sentences they exchanged were stilted and formal, and usually concerned the proposed holiday tour. At one point, Lacey remarked with some acerbity that if they were going to include the trek in the tour, then they had better provide a guide as well as porters, since it wasn't very likely that their clients would appreciate getting totally lost as she and Marcus had done. Marcus glanced up sharply, seemed about to say something equally cutting, then abruptly stopped himself and instead smoothly agreed with her.

They managed to get a flight back to England without any problems. After they had landed at the airport and retrieved their luggage, Marcus overrode Lacey's stubborn insistence that she could easily get a taxi, and drove her back to her flat himself. He parked the car, took her cases out of the boot, then stood there for a moment, a dark frown marking his face.

'I think it would be best if you didn't come in to work on Monday,' he said at last, rather harshly. 'We both need a bit of space, we can't seem to think straight when we're near each other. Do you understand what I'm saying, Lacey?'

Oh, yes, I understand! she thought to herself with some bitterness. Take a few days off—and try to find a new job in that time, because that'll solve everyone's problems very neatly.

She picked up her case, and fiercely shook her head when he offered to carry it in for her. She didn't need anyone's help—and especially not his.

The brief flare of defiance carried her through the front door of the flat, and got her as far as the tiny sitting-room. Then, without any warning, it suddenly disintegrated. As she collapsed on to the sofa, everything seemed too much for her to cope with any more, and she just sat there numbly staring at the floor.

Her flat-mate, Jane, came waltzing in from work a couple of hours later and found her still sitting there.

'Hello,' Jane greeted her cheerfully. 'I didn't expect you back for another couple of days yet. Have a good trip? What was it like, roaming all round India and Nepal with the gorgeous Marcus Caradin? Quite an experience, I bet!' Then she saw Lacey's face, her bright grin disappeared and a worried frown took its place. 'Lacey?' she said anxiously. 'What on earth's happened?' Then comprehension slowly dawned, and she gave a disbelieving groan. 'Oh, no! You didn't—you *couldn't* have fallen for him. Not you, Lacey, you're too sensible. You're the only one who never mooned over him every time he walked into the office, you laughed at us when we got all gooey-eyed over him——'

'Well, I'm not laughing now,' Lacey muttered in a muffled voice.

Jane sighed. 'I still don't believe it.' Her eyes opened a little wider. 'What on earth are you going to tell Robert?'

'Robert?' Lacey echoed blankly.

Jane shook her head in near despair. 'You have got it bad! Robert—the man you've been going out with for the last few months. Remember?'

'Oh, yes—Robert,' Lacey murmured listlessly. 'I don't think I'll be seeing him again.'

"You're not in a fit state to talk about this right now,' Jane decided. 'You'd better have a hot drink, then go straight to bed.'

'I won't be able to sleep.'

'You'll sleep,' predicted Jane confidently, and she was right, Lacey went out like a light just seconds after her head hit the pillow.

In the morning, she felt slightly less tired, but there was definitely no improvement in her emotional state. She crawled down to breakfast, ignored Jane's advice to go straight back to bed, then tried to eat. She couldn't, though, the food just wouldn't go down. All she could manage was a few sips of orange juice.

'You've certainly got all the symptoms,' sighed Jane. 'Any chance of the situation working itself out? I mean, I don't want to pry, but is this a strictly one-way thing, or is Marcus Caradin in the same state as you?'

'It's not very likely, is it?' Lacey replied, with a grimace. 'I mean, can you imagine him looking lovesick and forlorn?'

'No I can't,' admitted Jane, with a faint grin. Then she looked more serious again. 'Want to talk about it?' she invited quietly.

Lacey shrugged. 'There's not much to say. The whole

situation was a stalemate, right from the very beginning.
He doesn't want to get involved, he won't *let* himself get
involved. And at first, I felt exactly the same way. But
then I got to know him better, I realised he wasn't the sort
of man I thought he was. And by the time it dawned on
me that I was starting to like the real Marcus Caradin, it
was already too late, somewhere along the way I went the
whole hog and fell in love with him. Pretty stupid thing to
do, eh?' she shrugged, with a poor attempt at humour.

'What are you going to do about it?'

'The sensible thing, I suppose,' Lacey answered
tiredly. 'After all, that's what I'm meant to be so good at,
isn't it? Being sensible?' She rubbed her aching forehead.
'I can't make definite decisions right now. The weekend's coming up, I'll try and get some rest, then make
my mind up when I feel a bit better.'

'A bad attack of love isn't going to disappear over the
weekend,' Jane warned.

But Lacey didn't need anyone to tell her that, she had
already worked it out for herself. Marcus had been right,
though, she did need some space, some time to herself to
try and get everything straightened out. The only thing
that was worrying her was, how long was it going to take?
She found herself wishing her mother were near by, so
that she could go round and talk to her. Then she
grimaced ruefully. It probably wouldn't have been much
use anyway, she could guess the advice her mother would
instantly dole out. Go straight out and find another man,
there are plenty of them around, and replacements are
never too hard to find. Well, that solution might have
worked perfectly well for her mother, but Lacey was
beginning to suspect that Marcus Caradin was going to
be a difficult, perhaps even an impossible man to
replace.

All day Saturday she roamed around the flat feeling restless and depressed. Every time the phone rang, her heart would start to smash painfully against her ribs, then another black wave of depression would wash over her when the voice on the other end didn't turn out to be the one she wanted to hear. She still couldn't eat, it was hard enough even to drink, and at night she closed her eyes but didn't sleep.

On Sunday morning, she finally reached a decision. There was no way she could go back to work at Caradin Tours, so she might as well make a clean break right now. She had quite a few personal items in her desk, so she would go and clear them out, then she wouldn't have to set foot in the building ever again. She had her own set of keys that would let her into the office, and since it was Sunday, there was no chance of running into anyone and having to give a lot of awkward explanations.

She took a taxi to the small, modern office-block that housed Caradin Tours, used her special key that switched off the burglar-alarm system, then let herself into the building. It seemed strange to see it silent and deserted, instead of full of people working flat out. She didn't linger, though, instead she headed straight for her own office.

It took her only minutes to empty her desk. For a short while afterwards, she just stood there looking around her rather blankly. Then she gave herself a quick mental shake, and was just about to leave again when she heard the echo of footsteps heading purposefully in her direction.

She froze to the spot; she didn't even want to think about who it might be. Yet when Marcus walked through the door she found she wasn't surprised, it was almost as if she had been expecting him. All the same, seeing him in the flesh was a fairly nerve-shattering experience; a great surge of memories rolled over her and left her shaking, she could remember the taste and touch of him, and her body shivered in recognition of its own instinctive response to him.

And for a few moments, he seemed no less shaken. The grey eyes definitely weren't remote or soulless, instead they burned with a deep intensity. Then he came to an abrupt halt a few feet away from her, as if he didn't trust himself to come any closer.

'What are you doing here?' she said in a low voice.

'I went round to your flat, to see you, but Jane said you'd come here, to clear out your things. Running away?' he challenged softly.

The unfairness of that accusation briefly choked her. '*You* were the one who told me you didn't want me coming back here again,' she reminded him harshly, when she finally found her voice.

He shook his head. 'Wrong, Lacey. I just said that we needed a brief break from each other.'

'Then why are you here?' she demanded. 'It's only a couple of days since we flew back home, we've been apart hardly any time at all.'

'That's true,' he agreed. 'But it didn't take me very long to find out that I didn't like being separated from you for even a few hours, let alone days. It's rather ironic, don't you think?' he mused. 'I've spent the last couple of weeks trying to get away from you, and when I finally managed it I was as miserable as hell. So I decided to do something about it.'

She looked at him edgily. 'Like what?'

'We'll get to that later,' he told her cheerfully. 'First of all, I'd like to know how you feel about a couple of things.'

'What sort of things?' Lacey asked guardedly.

'Nothing very complicated,' he assured her. 'For a start—do you suppose you could get used to the idea of marrying me?'

And his voice might have been light, but there was certainly nothing casual about the expression on his face, and his eyes had just darkened several shades.

Lacey shook her head dazedly; it was about the last thing on earth she had been expecting, and it was impossible to believe that he had actually meant it. 'But you said——' she began jerkily.

'I know what I said,' Marcus agreed. 'And I certainly meant it at the time, I was determined not to get involved in a relationship where I wasn't totally in control. Only I've found that I *like* not being in control where you're concerned,' he went on, his voice suddenly husky. 'I like it very much.'

But she had been through too much, she couldn't accept that there could be such a dramatic change virtually overnight. She wanted to believe it—my God, how much!—but she had already convinced herself that miracles didn't happen, at least not to her.

She lifted her head and studied him warily. 'Nothing's changed,' she warned him at last. 'We're the same two people we were a few days ago, when you were convinced it wouldn't work out between us. All the old problems are still there, they haven't just miraculously vanished.'

A faint frown touched Marcus's face. 'One thing's changed,' he reminded her a little sharply. 'We made love. And don't tell me that didn't make any difference,' he added with unexpected fierceness.

'Why not?' she flung back at him, with a first touch of anger. 'It certainly didn't seem to make much difference to you! In fact, next morning you behaved as if the whole thing had been some dreadful mistake.'

Marcus gave a deep grimace, as if he would have preferred not to remember his behaviour on that particular day. 'You know me well enough by now to know that I'm a stubborn bastard. Something inside me still wouldn't let go, I suppose I went on fighting you out of sheer habit. If you take me on, you're going to have to get used to the fact that I can be very bloody-minded at times.'

'I realised that a long time ago,' she retorted, but her tone was a fraction softer now, and her eyes weren't quite so shadowed as they had been moments ago.

Marcus looked at her intently. 'Look, Lacey, I don't know what it is between us, I don't understand it and I certainly can't explain it, I just know that it's there. For a start, we talk—oh sure,' he went on wryly, 'a lot of the time we argue, and I don't suppose that's going to change, but in between times we communicate. I've told you things that I didn't think I'd ever tell anyone. And the physical fireworks are there, but it goes a lot deeper than that. I don't just want to take you to bed, I want to *be* with you.' He paused briefly. 'With my track-record, I don't blame you for being wary about saying yes to a long-term commitment,' he went on quietly. 'Do you want a written guarantee that it's going to last for ever? I can't give you that. I don't suppose anyone could. But somewhere deep inside me, I know we can make it if we really want to.' His gaze caught and held hers. 'Do you want to, Lacey?' he asked evenly.

'Yes, I want to,' she admitted in a small voice. 'But——'

'You don't like the type of man I am?' he said, in a voice that had suddenly gone rather grim.

Lacey instantly shook her head. 'No, it's not that. It

was a problem at the beginning,' she admitted. 'For a long while, I thought you were like the men my mother always went for, the type I always detested. Smooth, sophisticated, full of charm, incredibly good in bed——'

'And now you've found out I'm none of those things?' commented Marcus drily.

She flushed, but then gave a faint grin. 'You're all that—and a lot more!'

'Then what's the problem?' He gave a light frown. 'Perhaps it's that you don't trust me?' he suggested.

She shook her head again. 'It's not that either. It's just that I can't quite seem to get used to the idea—it's all a bit sudden——'

'You did say that you loved me,' he reminded her.

A surge of colour rushed over her. 'And you didn't like it!' she retaliated.

Unexpectedly, he grinned. 'No, I didn't. But that was because I wanted to say the same thing right back to you. And considering how hard I'd been fighting the fact that I was falling in love with you, it threw me right off balance—and at a very inconvenient moment, if I remember rightly.'

She went even redder. She remembered, too!

'Somehow, it all started that morning at Varanasi,' Marcus went on, as he moved a little closer. 'Remember how I told you the Hindu pilgrims believe the river and the sun unite at dawn, and that it cleanses them both bodily and spiritually? I don't share those beliefs, but I can't help thinking something happened to *me* at that moment. I could almost feel something starting to change inside me; it felt as if everything was slowly beginning to come right at long last. Oh, I went on fighting it for a long time,' he admitted wryly. 'It's not easy to face up to the fact that your personal life's been a complete disaster to date, and that it's going to take a lot of drastic changes to try and put it right. But at least I know exactly what I want now, and that's a start, it gives me something to build on.' He paused briefly. 'I want *you*, Lacey,' he told her a little thickly.

'When did you realise all this?' she asked him slowly.

'Only hours after I'd dropped you at your flat,' he admitted. 'But I'd already booked myself into a private clinic for a complete medical check-up by then, and they didn't let me out again until just a couple of hours ago, so I didn't have a chance to tell you sooner.'

Her eyes immediately fixed on his face with some alarm. 'What did they say about the concussion, the amnesia?'

'According to the doctors, there's no reason why the amnesia should come back, now it's cleared up. And they couldn't find anything wrong with my head except for some slight swelling and bruising that should soon disappear.' Marcus grinned. 'It's probably my thick skull that saved me from being more badly hurt. They did say, though, that it wouldn't hurt to have a week of complete rest. In fact, they actually recommended that I should stay in bed for the first couple of days. The only trouble is,' he continued meaningfully, 'I'd be bored to death if I were on my own.'

Lacey had finally begun to relax just a fraction, and now she allowed herself to lift one eyebrow. 'Well, I dare say you could always rustle up a tall blonde from somewhere,' she remarked a little caustically.

His gaze rested on her with some thoughtfulness. 'Is that remark meant to be significant?'

Her mouth set in a rather prim line. 'It's just that you were seen at a night club with a gorgeous blonde. And according to all the rumours, she's just one of an absolute harem.'

Marcus's eyebrows shot up. 'Are you jealous?' he queried, sounding faintly astonished, and yet unexpectedly pleased.

'Certainly not!' Lacey denied at once. Then her gaze sidled back to him. 'Should I have been?' she countered cautiously.

His mouth twitched. 'I was definitely at the club with a tall, gorgeous blonde,' he confirmed. Then, seeing her face, he added quickly, 'But she happened to be my sister, Ellen. It was her birthday, and her husband had to go abroad at the last minute on a business trip, so she was feeling pretty depressed. I took her out for the evening to try and cheer her up.'

'Your sister?' echoed Lacey, instantly looking much happier.

'I'll take you to meet her fairly soon,' Marcus promised. 'I think the two of you will get along very well, you're both beautiful and argumentative and well worth loving. And about this harem of women,' he added drily. 'It's very flattering that everyone should think I'm so irresistible to the female sex, but I have to admit the whole thing only exists in other people's imagination. I'd be the first to agree that I've not exactly led a celibate life, but very few men do. And in future, my love-life is going to be even more restricted. The only woman I'm ever going to want in my bed is you. So how about it, Lacey?' he prompted a little huskily. 'You still haven't given me an answer to my proposal. How much longer are you going to make me wait?'

But it was still incredibly difficult to believe that any of this was really happening, she just couldn't seem to get out the one short word he was waiting to hear.

'Never mind,' he went on in a relaxed tone, moving still closer until he was within touching distance, 'we've got plenty of time. And I could have a lot of fun persuading you to give me the right answer.'

While he was talking, he reached out for her, and Lacey was rather alarmed to find his hands had already begun to wander over her with bold confidence, taking a lot of pleasure in reacquainting themselves with the soft curves of her body. She swallowed hard, and felt herself beginning to succumb to the sweet magic that he was so expert at conjuring up.

'Mmm, gorgeous,' Marcus murmured appreciatively. 'You did say you were going to marry me, didn't you?'

Her breathing seemed to be packing up completely. 'I don't think I actually said it,' she gasped rather faintly.

'Then perhaps I ought to work on it a little harder,' came his thoughtful reply. 'It shouldn't be too difficult to squeeze that one small word out of you. Y-e-s—it won't take you any time to say it. I'll show you just how easy it can be,' he promised huskily.

His busy fingers brought a fresh flush of colour to her already glowing skin. A couple more minutes of this, she thought wildly, and she would be ready to promise him anything!

'Of course, this is bound to make a difference to our working relationship,' he went on, a few moments later.

'I didn't know we had a working relationship any more,' Lacey mumbled. 'After all, you've spent the last couple of weeks trying to persuade me to find another job.'

'I still think that's rather a good idea,' he replied, making her head shoot up in fresh astonishment. 'I don't want you working as my secretary any longer. Instead, I

want you working *with* me,' he went on, his eyes glinting
with amusement at her startled reaction. 'I've got several
more trips abroad planned for this year, new holiday
tours to set up and organise, and I certainly don't intend
to go alone.' He paused to explore a particularly sensitive
patch of her skin, making her shiver involuntarily. 'It
was very thoughtful of you to wear a dress that buttons
down the front,' he told her, briefly getting side-tracked.
'You really do have beautiful breasts. Did I tell you that
before?' One finger explored their outline with obvious
pleasure. 'How would you like to honeymoon in China?'
he added.

It was several seconds before his last remark sank in,
she was floating in a pool of pure pleasure now. Her
heavy eyelids finally fluttered open, though, and she
blinked at him rather dazedly.

'China?' she echoed.

'It's a fascinating country,' he assured her. 'You'll love
it. And we'll spend a few days in Hong Kong on the way
home.'

'I don't like travelling,' she responded automatically,
but somehow there wasn't very much conviction in her
voice.

'We've been through all this before,' Marcus replied
patiently. 'You don't really want a quiet, dull life—you
want the kind of life that you'll have with me.'

And he was right, of course. A small part of her was
already eagerly looking forward to exploring the world
with him. But she didn't intend to tell him that just yet,
she was beginning to enjoy the novel sensation of having
the upper hand where Marcus Caradin was concerned.
And because she suspected that it would turn out to be a
fairly rare position to be in, she intended to make the
most of it.

He had other ideas, though, his clever fingers had already found the catch on her bra, and now he had bent his head so that his lips could tease the dark pink tip of one aching breast. 'I'm still waiting for an answer, Lacey,' he reminded her, his voice not quite as steady as it had been only moments ago.

'That isn't fair,' she protested weakly. 'It's practically blackmail!'

'Whatever it takes,' came his slightly muffled response as he ruthlessly followed up his advantage until she was reduced to a puddle of melting delight. 'I gave you a bad time, but now I intend to make up for it. I want it to be legal, though. I'll be the first to admit I'm not ideal husband material, but I do love you, Lacey, and I'll try like hell to get it right. So—are you going to say yes?' His tongue licked moistly, sensuously, against her hot, quivering skin. '*Are* you?'

A small shiver of surrender swept through her. 'Yes,' she muttered in a strangled voice.

A smile of pure triumph lifted the corners of Marcus's mouth. Then he returned to the gentle nibbling that was driving her a little crazy, not stopping until she actually groaned out loud. Only then did he relent, easing up on those small, killingly pleasurable caresses.

'And what exactly are you agreeing to?' he asked a little huskily. 'To marrying me? Or to something else?'

'To anything,' Lacey responded helplessly.

His hands slid into her hair, they stroked the glossy red strands, then dug themselves in even deeper, pulling her nearer.

'We're going to have a fantastic marriage if you carry on being so amenable and accommodating,' he murmured. Then his eyes went still darker, and he drew in a rather unsteady breath. 'It's Sunday,' he reminded her.

'We've got the place to ourselves, no one's going to walk in and disturb us. And there's a very comfortable sofa in my office.' His hands left her hair and instead locked on to the small of her back, holding her tightly against him, making her aware of his achingly deep arousal. 'You see what you do to me?' he accused. 'You've only got to walk into a room and I start wanting you. Come any closer, and I start to fall apart.'

Lacey looked up at him and suddenly grinned. 'You did force me to say yes,' she reminded him. 'Who knows what else you could force me to do if you really put your mind to it?'

'I don't want to force you into anything,' he growled.

'I'm not actually struggling,' she pointed out. 'And if you slung me over your shoulder and carried me off, I wouldn't mind betting you wouldn't hear a single squeak of protest.'

One eyebrow shot up. 'So you go for the caveman approach? But I don't like any rough stuff, Lacey,' he told her throatily. 'I like it to be slow and subtle and very, very good.' Yet an instant later, she found herself swept off her feet and swung up into his arms. 'On the other hand,' he went on a little breathlessly, 'I'm always willing to try anything once.'

'Or twice?' she prompted mischievously.

'Or even three times—if I've got the stamina,' he added drily. Then his face changed, his eyes gleamed fiercely. 'But however it turns out, just remember that I love you, I intend to marry you, and it'll always be good between us. I promise you that, Lacey.'

And she believed him, and was content to stay curled up in his arms, letting him carry her off to the glittering future that stretched out ahead of them.

Harlequin Presents

Coming Next Month

1119 COMPARATIVE STRANGERS Sara Craven
Nigel's betrayal had shattered Amanda's dreams of their happy life together.
She doesn't know where to turn until Malory, Nigel's elder brother, takes
charge. He's a virtual stranger to her, yet she finds herself agreeing to
marry him!

1120 LOVE IN A MIST Sandra Field
A disastrous early marriage had brought Sally a small daughter she adored but
left her wary about love and commitment. It was ironic that trying to make a
new start on a holiday on St. Pierre she should meet attractive Luke Sheridan.
He felt exactly the same way she did....

1121 HEART OF THE HAWK Sandra Marton
As a step-aunt with skimpy earnings, Rachel has no legal chance of keeping her
nephew when his wealthy father comes to claim him. She discovers why David
Griffin is called The Hawk—and begins to realize the complications facing her.

1122 TRIAL OF INNOCENCE Anne Mather
Throughout her marriage to Stephen Morley, Robyn kept her guilty secret.
And she has no intention of revealing the truth now—even though Stephen is
dead and his brother, Jared, is asking questions that demand answers!

1123 TOO MUCH TO LOSE Susanne McCarthy
Jessica doesn't deserve her reputation as a scarlet woman, but finds it
impossible to set the record straight. Not that she cares what people think,
especially Sam Ryder. She needs him to save her business—that's the only
reason he's in her life.

1124 TAKE THIS WOMAN Lilian Peake
Kirsten is surprised when she inherits her late employer's country mansion.
She's even more surprised to find herself attracted to his great-nephew, Scott
Baird—especially when Scott wants to ruin all her plans and dreams.

1125 IMPOSSIBLE BARGAIN Patricia Wilson
Money is all that matters to Merissa—for the best of reasons. But Julian
Forrest doesn't know them and promptly jumps to all the wrong conclusions
about her. So why should he want her to pose as his fiancée?

1126 SHADOWS ON BALI Karen van der Zee
Nick Donovan broke Megan's heart two years ago when he plainly rejected her.
Now, meeting again, they're forced to work together on the same project in
Bali. And to Megan's disgust, Nick expects her to behave as if nothing had
happened!

Available in November wherever paperback books are sold, or through
Harlequin Reader Service:

In the U.S.
901 Fuhrmann Blvd.
P.O. Box 1397
Buffalo, N.Y. 14240-1397

In Canada
P.O. Box 603
Fort Erie, Ontario
L2A 5X3

Take 4 books
& a surprise gift
FREE

SPECIAL LIMITED-TIME OFFER

Mail to   **Harlequin Reader Service** ®

In the U.S.   In Canada
901 Fuhrmann Blvd.   P.O. Box 609
P.O. Box 1867   Fort Erie, Ontario
Buffalo, N.Y. 14269-1867   L2A 5X3

YES!   Please send me 4 free Harlequin Temptation® novels
and my free surprise gift. Then send me 4 brand-new novels every
month as they come off the presses. Bill me at the low price of
$2.24 each*—a 10% saving off the retail price. There are no
shipping, handling or other hidden costs. There is no minimum
number of books I must purchase. I can always return a shipment
and cancel at any time. Even if I never buy another book from
Harlequin, the 4 free novels and the surprise gift are mine to keep
forever.   142 BPX BP7F

*Plus 49¢ postage and handling per shipment in Canada.

_____
Name   (PLEASE PRINT)

_____
Address   Apt. No.

_____
City   State/Prov.   Zip/Postal Code

This offer is limited to one order per household and not valid to present
subscribers. Price is subject to change.   DOHT-SUB-1C

Taylor House

by Leigh Anne Williams

Enter the lives of the Taylor women of Greensdale, Massachusetts, a town where tradition and family mean so much. A story of family, home and love in a New England village.

Don't miss the Taylor House trilogy, starting next month in Harlequin American Romance with #265 *Katherine's Dream*, in October 1988, and followed by #269 *Lydia's Hope* and #273 *Clarissa's Wish* in November and December of 1988.

One house . . . two sisters . . . three generations

ATTRACTIVE, SPACE SAVING BOOK RACK

Display your most prized novels on this handsome and sturdy book rack. The hand-rubbed walnut finish will blend into your library decor with quiet elegance, providing a practical organizer for your favorite hard-or soft-covered books.

Only $9.95

Approximately 16" x 8" when assembled

Assembles in seconds!

To order, rush your name, address and zip code, along with a check or money order for $10.70* ($9.95 plus 75¢ postage and handling) payable to *Harlequin Reader Service*:

Harlequin Reader Service
Book Rack Offer
901 Fuhrmann Blvd.
P.O. Box 1396
Buffalo, NY 14269-1396

Offer not available in Canada.

BKR-1A

*New York and Iowa residents add appropriate sales tax.